**Jason tried not to pay attention
to the crumbling of the path under his feet.**

His fingers flew over the dials. The vibrations beneath him were so violent that his hand continually slipped.

"Hurry!" shouted Gwen.

"I am!"

"Hurry!"

"I am!"

Jason twisted the last dial, and with a noise that sounded like smoothly turning gears, the door slid up into the ceiling. Immediately, Gwen, Jason, and Booj leaped into the opening—just as the path behind them fell completely apart.

They stood on the other side of the door and breathed a sigh of relief. "That was close," said Jason.

And then, without warning, the path on the other side of the door crumbled beneath their feet, dumping them into blackness. Just like that, they were gone.

VISIT THE EXCITING WORLD OF

IN THESE BOOKS:

Windchaser by Scott Ciencin

River Quest by John Vornholt

Hatchling by Midori Snyder

Lost City by Scott Ciencin

Sabertooth Mountain by John Vornholt

Thunder Falls by Scott Ciencin

Firestorm by Gene DeWeese

The Maze by Peter David

AND COMING SOON:

Rescue Party by Mark A. Garland

DINOTOPIA®
THE MAZE

by Peter David

Random House ⌂ New York

To Gwen, Cayley, and other adventurers everywhere
—P.D.

The publisher's special thanks to
James Gurney, Scott Usher,
and project adviser on paleontology,
Dr. Michael Brett-Surman

THE MAZE

Windy Point

Crystal Caverns

The Hatchery

Baz

Pooktook

Volcaneum

Polongo River

Cornucopia
Treetown

Deep Lake

Bent Root

NORTHERN PLAINS

CRACKSHELL POINT

Temple Ruins

BACKBONE MOUNTAINS

Rocky Pass

Prosperine

Sapphire Bay

Poseidos
(sunken)

*Hadro
Swamp*

RAINY

BASIN

Waterfall City

GREAT CANAL

SKY GALLEY CAVES

Tentpole of the Sky

Sculpted Cliffs

Sky City

Thermala

The Time Towers

Sauropolis

Dolphin Bay

Canyon City

Ancient Gorge

*Red Rapid
Canyon*

The Portal

FORBIDDEN MOUNTAINS

Amu River

Pteros

The Sentinels

Warmwater
Bay

Culebra

OUTER ISLAND

GREAT DESERT

Dragonfly Coast

BLACKWOOD

FLATS

Chandara

Cape Turtletail

CHAPTER 1

The quartz crystals were large, sharp, and falling like hailstones—and that was the good news.

Gwen had always been fairly slim. Never was she more happy of that fact than at this particular moment. She twisted every which way, narrowly avoiding the crystals as they came clattering down.

Her only means of escape was a narrow bridge that dangled about fifty feet over a field of hardened red lava. The bridge looked none too sturdy—a fact that was not lost on her two companions.

Jason was tall and gawky. His piercing blue eyes displayed an intelligence that made him seem far older than his fourteen years. Next to Jason was Booj. Anywhere else in the world, Booj would have seemed an odd companion. Actually, anywhere else in the world, Booj would have seemed an impossible companion.

Booj was a Velociraptor. At ten feet long, he was larger than average. Perched somewhat awkwardly on his muscular legs, he stepped delicately among the rocks now sliding beneath his clawed feet.

Gwen had greenish brown eyes and long brown hair that cascaded around her shoulders. Normally, she was rather proud of her hair, but now it was covered with soot and dirt and kept getting into her eyes. If she'd had a knife, she would gladly have hacked it away.

When Booj and Jason first approached the bridge, they had miraculously managed not to trip the booby trap. But Gwen had accidentally stepped on the small pedal camouflaged in the ground, which had brought the quartz crystals cascading from a chute overhead.

Above them was a cavernous ceiling, and around them was a vast, underground, miles-long and miles-deep grotto with rocky walls and floors.

In the ceiling, a round section had slid aside, and Gwen had barely had time to shout a warning before the lethal shards started shooting down at them in clusters of ten at a time.

Booj and Jason had already jumped clear of them by a couple of feet, but the shards were blocking the narrow path ahead and Gwen remained in the line of fire. She threw her arms up over her head as she dodged the quartz crystals, listening to Jason's shouts, "There! There! No, there! Wait, over there!" as one overhead hole closed up and another opened.

"We've got to get out of here!" shouted Gwen.

"No kidding!" Jason replied, pointing to the bridge swaying in front of them. It was only about twenty feet across, but it certainly looked like the longest twenty feet that Gwen had ever seen. "But do you think that's going to hold us?"

"Looks like a fossil-maker for sure," Booj squawked in an awkward saurian tongue. Then he added with his customary cheerfulness, "But this is no problem. No problem at all. I will go first."

"Why you?" asked Jason. But before Booj could offer his response, another section of the ceiling opened up directly above Gwen. Jason quickly shoved her flat against the opposite side of the rock wall just as ten more crystals speared down on the area where she'd been standing a moment before. She breathed a grateful "Thanks" to him.

Booj cleared his throat and continued. "I am the heaviest. If it supports my weight, it will certainly hold you as well."

Without waiting for further discussion, Booj ran out onto the bridge. Heedless of its swaying, he calmly navigated the structure.

Gwen, in the meantime, was looking down at what awaited them should they fall off the bridge. The red ground below seemed to shimmer in the heat. "I can't say that I'm thrilled about the fall, but if we did fall, at least it would be onto cooled lava instead of molten," she said.

Jason shook his head. "It's still superheated. If you touch it, you'll get incinerated."

"Oh," said Gwen.

"Excuse me!" Booj interrupted.

They tore their attention away from the possibly devastating drop and spotted Booj on the far side of the crevice. He was looking rather pleased with himself. With a nod of his head, he gestured that they should follow. "Come! Hurry!" Booj squawked.

Jason put a tentative foot on the bridge and said to Gwen, "I'll go next, then you follow."

"No," whispered Gwen. She felt almost paralyzed with fear.

"All right," he said, sounding remarkably reasonable. "You go next, then I'll follow."

"Jason, I..." She looked at him helplessly, angry at her own weakness. "I'm afraid of heights. And it doesn't look very strong. And I—Jason, don't ask me to do this."

"You don't have a choice, Gwen. Do you want your father to die? Now come on and move!" he suddenly shouted, reaching out and grabbing her hand. He yanked her toward him, and she slammed into him with such force that they both almost fell off the edge. Just then, another barrage of shards blasted downward, chewing up the rock that surrounded them. They were rapidly running out of space.

"Do you want your father to die?" Jason demanded again, and then added, "Do you want *you* to die? Because that's what's going to happen if we stay here. You die, your father dies. And our entire mission becomes a pointless failure. Now, what's it going to be, Gwen?"

She sighed, knowing he was right. "You go first,"

she told him. "You go, and I'll follow."

Jason nodded, then turned and bolted across the bridge. The bridge rattled under his feet but otherwise remained solid. Once he arrived on the other side, he turned and called to her, "See? No problem!" He gestured hurriedly. "Come on!"

"Yeah, you can do it!" squawked Booj.

Gwen took a deep breath. She shuddered as her lungs filled with the heat of the lava from below. Then she heard a sound, a sort of *ka-chunk* noise. Immediately, she knew what it was: a new barrage of quartz crystals was coming. She couldn't hesitate any longer. She gathered her strength and pushed herself off from the edge.

The quartz crystals hurtled down behind her as she raced forward. Several shards struck the rope supports that kept the bridge taut.

The ropes snapped!

The bridge dropped from under Gwen's feet. She let out a frantic shriek that drowned out the alarmed cries of Booj and Jason. With only a split second to act, she lunged forward, throwing herself flat against the remains of the bridge in front of her.

The bridge swung downward and slammed against the far rock wall, where one end was still anchored. The impact almost knocked her off completely, but she clung to the side with all the determination her fingers could find.

As Gwen dangled halfway between the safety of

the ground above and the hardened lava beneath, the heat became even more intense. She felt her lungs straining against it. She was suffocating, and she knew it. Exerting all her strength, Gwen began to haul herself up, one plank at a time. Jason and Booj shouted encouragement as she pulled herself up a foot, then two feet, and then three.

"That's it!" shouted Jason. "You can do it!"

Four feet, then five, and the heat was receding just a bit.

And then a plank, already weakened by the impact of hitting the wall, snapped. Just like that, Gwen started to plummet toward the lava, her arms waving wildly. After falling several feet, somehow she managed to grab a plank with one hand while her other arm dangled desperately.

The heat from below was draining every bit of moisture from her body. Her breath became hard and ragged in her chest. Her face was covered with soot. She couldn't even muster the strength to bring her other arm around.

"Booj, quick! Your tail!" Jason cried out.

Booj sank his claws into the ground and dangled his long tail over the edge. "Grab it, Gwen!" Jason called. "You can do it! Grab his tail!"

Gwen tried to reach it with her free hand. But she could only flail about, her strength rapidly dwindling to nothingness. No matter how much Booj stretched it, his tail remained just out of reach.

"I'm—I'm sorry, Daddy," she whispered through cracked lips, though her father was miles away and couldn't hear her.

"Booj, hold on tight!" Jason said suddenly.

"Why? What are you going to—?"

Before Booj could react, Jason leaped off the edge. He grabbed Booj's tail and slid down it. "Gwen!" he shouted.

She barely realized he was there. As her fingers started to slip off the edge of the plank, Jason lunged downward, reaching for her with such a violent move that he almost lost his hold on Booj's tail.

Jason's hand snagged Gwen's wrist just as her exhausted grip let go of the plank. They were now both dangling above the lava. Gwen knew she was dead weight. She felt weak and dizzy, and she knew, at this moment, that their lives depended on the fastness of Jason's hold on her and the durability of the Raptor's tail.

It was, to put it mildly, something of a strain on the dinosaur. The weight was clearly overwhelming for Booj. He grunted and growled deep in his throat. Then Jason shouted, "You have to pull us up! It's up to you, Booj!"

"Up to me," muttered the Raptor. "Thanks a lot."

Gwen could picture Booj pushing forward with his powerful legs. She heard his claws scraping and digging into place with each new step forward. He moved slowly, clearly taking extra care to proceed as smoothly as possible, because the slightest abrupt movement might cause Jason to lose his hold and send both of them falling to their deaths.

It seemed that the entire ordeal took hours, but it was barely a minute before Jason's head lifted above the edge of the cliff. "That's it!" shouted Jason. "That's it, Booj! You're doing it! Just a little farther! That's it!"

"I know you think you're shouting encouragement," Booj squawked, "but the fact is that you're distracting me something fierce. So let me concentrate here, okay?"

Jason promptly lapsed into silence, and Booj silently kept hauling. The only sounds to be heard were Booj's claws scraping against the rock and, every so often, a low grunt from the Raptor.

Then, suddenly, the ground was there. Gwen saw Booj quickly crane his neck to verify that she and Jason were indeed safe on the edge of the cliff.

Except...now Gwen wasn't feeling like she could keep her eyes open....

"Gwen isn't moving!" Jason's voice shouted. "She—I don't think—she's not breathing!"

Gwen was barely aware of what Jason was saying. She wasn't even sure of where she was anymore. The heat from the lava had completely drained her, and she felt herself slipping away.

The simple act of breathing seemed too much trouble for Gwen, and part of her mind told her to stop doing it altogether. *Yes...yes. Just stop breathing.*

Take a rest from everything—from breathing, from hurting, from life—that's the way to go....

She heard Jason shouting, calling her name, but her thoughts were no longer on him, or on their mission. Instead, she felt her mind spiraling backward to two days ago, before her life had fallen apart. Back to her time on the farm, back before her father fell ill.

She had been so unhappy even then. But now, she wanted nothing more than to be back home with her dad.

CHAPTER 2

Eric Corey had wanted a son. His daughter, Gwen, had always known this, deep in her heart. Not that her father had ever said it, of course. But she knew it just the same because, somehow, daughters simply know these things.

It didn't help that she saw nothing of herself in him, nor he in her. Instead, he would always comment on how much she looked like her mother, particularly if she held her head in a certain way while the sun was setting, or if he noticed her simply staring off thoughtfully as her mother had often done.

Gwen wished with all her heart that she could have known her mother, that her mother had not died when Gwen had been a baby. Part of the reason she wished it was simple curiosity: she would have liked knowing the woman who had given her life. Another part of the reason was simple selfishness: if her mother had lived, she might have had a brother, and her father wouldn't have spent so many days looking at her with thinly disguised disappointment.

At least, that's how Gwen saw it.

Her best friend, Cayley, thought she was crazy.

Cayley came to visit the Corey farm regularly. As farms went, it was somewhat small, and the area was more arid than Gwen's father would have liked, but he had a number of crops that produced year after year. He had always been a farmer, even in his native England, before he had come to Dinotopia.

He'd told Gwen the story many times. He had been on a trip to visit relatives in 1850 when a sudden and very fierce storm had sent his ship to the bottom of the ocean. He had thought that he would share the same fate, but then—miraculously—he had felt himself borne forward on the backs of what he at first believed were mermaids. When his confusion lifted, he realized that two dolphins had come to his aid. They had brought him to Dinotopia, an isolated, mysterious, and amazing place where sentient and knowledgeable dinosaurs shared their land, their work, and their lives with humans.

Eric Corey had met his wife, Margaret, several years after he'd arrived. He always said that the moment he saw her beautiful smile, he became a firm believer in fate.

It had nearly killed Eric when Margaret died. He was sick about it for weeks and might have died of a broken heart, were it not for his infant daughter Gwen needing him so desperately. So he had pulled himself together to do the best he could in raising her.

This was something that Cayley had pointed out to Gwen on more than one occasion. Cayley was as slim as Gwen, but with long strawberry blond hair, an inquisitive air, and a smattering of freckles across her face. She was the daughter of a shop owner in a nearby village and had become friendly with Gwen over the years.

"Your father's crazy about you," Cayley told Gwen one day. They were at their favorite meeting place, on the edge of a small pond in the nearby wood. "I hear the way he talks to you, the proud looks he gives you."

"I know, I know," Gwen replied, picking up a stone and tossing it so that it skipped across the pond's surface. "But when I see him at the end of the day, he just looks at me sadly across the dinner table. He always looks so tired. I just know he's thinking how much easier life around the farm would be if he had a son."

"He's got Dismo," Cayley pointed out.

Dismo was an elderly Triceratops who had always maintained a rather dour attitude. He and Gwen's father had first met through rather unusual circumstances: as competitors.

Doddering into his later years, Dismo had been seeking something to occupy his time. He had investigated a number of possibilities, but none of them were particularly attractive to him. The one pastime that had brought him any amusement was Triassic, a three-level game of strategy similar to chess.

A local competition drew Gwen's father, who was one of the top human players. It also drew Dismo, who was one of the leading dinosaur practitioners of the game, but none too enthused about it, since he rarely was enthused about anything. They played three times—one game to Dismo, the second to Eric Corey, and the third a draw. In that time they developed such an appreciation for each other's company that, once the competition was over, they were reluctant to go their separate ways.

"I have a farm and a daughter I really have to get back to," Eric had told Dismo.

"I," Dismo had replied, "do not have anyplace particular to go, and no one waiting for me."

Eric had paused, considering options, and had then said, "I could certainly use help on my farm. I can provide you with room and board and the occasional game of Triassic, if you're interested."

"I am not at all interested," Dismo had informed him. Then he paused and added, "When do we leave?"

That was how Dismo had come to reside on the Corey farm. Gwen hadn't quite known what to make of him at first, but she had come to accept and appreciate his presence. Dismo provided adult company for her father, and she could understand his need for that.

"Dismo isn't exactly a son, Cayley," Gwen said. "He's a friend. That's all." She tossed another stone into the pond. This one didn't skip. It sank. Gwen felt as though her spirits were tied to it.

"You shouldn't be so upset about this," Cayley told Gwen. "If you're really disturbed by it, if it really bothers you, then you should talk to your father about it. Confront him."

"He'd never admit to it."

"Maybe, maybe not. But at least he'll know how you feel."

"Okay," Gwen said slowly. "I'll ask him. I'm not sure how I'm going to do it, but I'll ask him."

That night, Gwen sat opposite her father at the dinner table. As usual, there was nothing to hear but the clattering of flatware and the sounds of chewing.

Her father wasn't much interested in what he termed "useless chatter." He oftentimes told her that words were like coins, not to be tossed around lest they be pointlessly wasted. Part of Gwen was convinced that she was about to waste her time, but she felt as if she had to take a shot at something.

"I've been thinking about irrigation lately, Dad," she said. Her voice seemed rather loud since it had been so quiet.

Eric Corey was tall and lean. He had a bald spot on the back of his head that had been spreading with each passing year. The hair that remained was turning gray. He looked thoughtful, his mind a million miles away. He glanced up at her, forcing himself to focus, pulling his mind away from whatever else had been occupying it. "We irrigate," he told her, sounding slightly confused that she would bring up such a topic.

"Yes, I know. I remember when Dismo helped dig the ditch so the water would flow down to the field."

"Well, then...?" His voice trailed off questioningly.

"Well, I was just thinking," she said "Our fields—they aren't exactly even. The ground goes up and down in all different places, so the irrigation is uneven. In some places there are huge puddles and it's oversoaked, and other places have barely enough to provide coverage. So, how about if we even out the grade? Level it somehow? Get enough dirt or something like that so that the land is level, and then we can—"

"The land is the land, Gwen," her father told her flatly. "We make do with what's given to us. Things are fine the way we do them now."

Then Gwen's father rose from his chair and carried his dishes over to the sink. Clearly that was the end of the discussion. Without even glancing over his shoulder, he said, "Do you want to wash tonight, or dry?"

Suddenly, everything bubbled up inside Gwen. She hadn't expected it to, hadn't realized that she was quite this angry. It happened almost before she knew it. She grabbed up the metal plate that was on the table before her and hurled it across the room. It sailed like a discus and ricocheted off the far wall, clattering to the floor. It made a considerable racket, and her father looked around at her in surprise.

"Gwen?" He wasn't even able to form a question, he was so surprised. Such behavior was unheard of for Gwen.

"You wanted a son, didn't you," she said tightly. "If I were a boy, you'd pay attention to me when I talk about ways of making things better on the farm. It's all because you've always wanted a son. I can tell...the way you look at me—or don't look at me. The way you always act like you'd rather be somewhere else when I'm around. You wish I were a boy, don't you? Don't you?"

It was the first time she had ever confronted her father directly. She wasn't sure how he was going to react. Whether he would yell or shake his fists or burst out in a flood of denial...or maybe even admit to it.

What she wasn't prepared for was a simple, noncommittal shrug.

"Children are no different than the land," he said. "We make do with what's given us."

"So I'm right," she said slowly.

He shook his head. "You're my daughter. I love you. Any other discussion is simply pointless. Dwelling on what might have been is a waste of time, Gwen. And there're not enough hours in the day for me to waste. I'm a farmer and I have other things to do."

"I thought…" Gwen's voice trailed off.

Then her father prompted, "You thought what, Gwen?"

"I thought we were farmers."

There was a long silence, the most crushing silence Gwen had ever felt. Her father reached down, picked up the plate she had thrown, quickly inspected it for damage, and then put it in the sink without a word.

Suddenly, Gwen felt as if she had to get out. She wasn't sure where, but she just knew she was going to suffocate in the small house. She bolted through the door, and even as she did, she waited for her father to call her name, to ask her to come back to him. But he didn't.

So Gwen ran until she was out of breath, until her house was just a small and distant speck, only the light of the hearth glowing through the window was visible. There was a sob in her chest, but she choked it back. The cool night air was stinging in her lungs.

She sat down, curling her knees up under her chin. *Why did things have to be this way?* she thought. *Why?*

Then she noticed something.

A pair of eyes was watching her from the nearby woods.

She blinked because she wasn't quite sure what she was seeing. The eyes appeared to be red and glowing. Her first thought was that it was a dinosaur, but she knew of no saurian whose eyes shone in such an unearthly fashion.

She had no idea how long the observer had been there, but she wasn't about to be intimidated. She cupped her hands around her mouth and called, "Hello! Who are you? I see you there! What are you doing hiding there in the woods?"

Unfortunately, she was not about to get an answer, because the possessor of those most curious eyes suddenly turned away. It was as if the watcher had simply vanished back into the shadows, hiding in them or maybe even merging with them.

She called several more times, but there was no reply. She momentarily considered entering the woods in pursuit of this odd stranger but realized that running around in the forest at night was a good way to do herself harm.

"Well, good night, then!" she called. Then she turned and headed back to what she was sure would be a very quiet and tense home.

As soon as she was gone, the red eyes floated into view once more.

CHAPTER 3

"Boooooj!"

Booj had come to know that particular bellow. It meant that, once again, he was in trouble. And it was precisely the sort of trouble that he loved.

The group of Velociraptors with whom he lived kept more or less to themselves. Many years ago they had established a settlement not too far from Volcaneum, where a dormant volcano was one of the major features of the area. The volcano had never represented a problem to those who lived there. At least, it hadn't until the day that Booj had staggered into the middle of the Raptor village.

Booj's farm, which was on the outskirts of the settlement, had been covered with some sort of thick, steaming mass that looked as if it had to be lava. Although the mass turned out to be completely harmless, Booj let out a long, piercing scream, pitched forward, and lay there, twitching. This had been enough to send almost every other Raptor in the village into a complete panic, convinced that they themselves were next. Frightened Raptors had started running this way and that while Booj tried not to burst into laughter.

He had not earned himself many friends that day. Actually, he didn't have all that many thereafter. As a matter of fact, he had precisely none.

"Boooooj!" came the angry bellow again.

Booj wasn't exactly sure what had gotten him into trouble this time. It could have been any number of things.

"Coming, your wonderfulness!" Booj called. He loped quickly through the Raptor village. Actually, "village" might have been too elaborate a word. By human standards it looked more like an encampment.

Gypsy-like, the Raptor village was mobile, moving from one place to the next whenever the urge struck them. Generally, they stuck to the area of Volcaneum, circling the perimeter of the huge volcano from which the territory derived its name.

Xin, the Elder of the settlement, was waiting for him. It seemed to Booj that Xin never hesitated to make his feelings about Booj's antics known. The moment the young Raptor appeared before him, Xin wasted no time. "Were you responsible, Booj?" he asked in their saurian tongue.

"For what, your graciousness?" Booj inquired, keeping as neutral a tone as possible.

"I think you know quite well," Xin said sternly. "The snare."

"Snare?"

"The one that Lafes stumbled into this morning. The one that yanked him twenty feet into the air and kept him dangling for two hours until we could find a way to cut him down."

"Oh, *that* snare," Booj said, scratching his snout thoughtfully. "I seem to recall hearing something about it, yes. That would be the same Lafes who was telling me the other day what a wasteful fool I am?"

"Lafes lost his temper, Booj! It happens! You did not have to retaliate in such a manner!"

"If you want to call it retaliation, Xin, you're certainly entitled to. Me, I call it a lesson. A lesson in paying attention to precisely where one walks. Otherwise one may just step blindly into something that puts one in a very *foolish* position."

Xin appeared to consider his next words very carefully, fighting for patience. "Booj, we are all very aware of how intelligent you are. You may be one of the brightest Raptors I have ever known. Certainly you're also one of the longest, from snout to tail; some find your stature a bit intimidating—not that I'm one of them, you understand."

"Of course not," Booj said diplomatically.

Xin continued, "Your ability for languages is astounding; your musical compositions seem as if they come to you from on high."

"But?"

"You alienate the others, Booj! You are like a

rolled-up scroll to us. We never know what to make of your behavior, with your pranks, your jokes, and your acting as if you are smarter than anyone else."

"I am," Booj said evenly.

"Perhaps you are! But there is a certain graciousness that should come with that, Booj. You have no humility."

"Why should I be humble?" Booj asked reasonably. "Do I have reason to be?"

"You don't care about anyone other than yourself."

The rebuke stung. "That's not true," Booj said. "I do care. I care about others. If I play pranks and such, well, that's my way of showing that I care."

"No, that is your way of showing that you are smarter. That, and your way of burning off 'claw energy.' We all have that, Booj. You, me, the others—we are hunters at heart, we have impulses that we need to burn off. And we do so in a variety of ways. But the way you have chosen...it is damaging to others, to the morale of the village as a whole."

Xin sighed. "You can be an asset to us. Deep down, I am positive of that. But, at present, you are not being an asset. You are going to have to make some hard decisions, Booj. You are going to have to decide what it is that you want out of life. And for that, I might suggest you take some time away, some time to explore and discover."

Booj couldn't quite believe it. "Are you saying I must leave? Even if I don't wish to?"

"No, of course not. I will not force you to do anything you do not wish, Booj," Xin said patiently. "That is not my way. But I want to encourage what is best for you and your growth. It is my belief that it will help you to spend some time on your own, to explore options, and to seek out others beyond our village. It might do you some good. Help you to focus your life. To see what you want out of it."

"And if I do not wish to leave?" Booj asked in a challenging tone.

"Then here you will stay," Xin admitted. "But if you want my honest opinion, Booj—or, for that matter, even if you don't—you are not going to be happy here. You are going to continue to make others unhappy. And you and I are going to have many more of these discussions. I do not know about you, but I am not especially looking forward to that."

"Neither am I," admitted Booj.

"Booj, there is something you must realize. Life is very much a maze. You are thrown into it with only the vaguest idea of where you are going. We, none of us, know what is around every corner, and every so often, we find ourselves stuck. Right now, Booj, I think you are stuck in the maze. All I am trying to do is give you a push in the right direction. Or at least what I believe is the right direction. It is up to you to choose the next turn.

"Just remember this. In my experience, those of us who do not remain stuck in life's maze are the ones who seek answers to where they should be going. If you do not work to discover this, Booj, you may find yourself forever getting stuck.

"Think about it, Booj," Xin finished kindly. "Think about it."

CHAPTER 4

The sun was blazing hot that day, and Eric Corey noticed that Dismo was pulling the plow more slowly than usual. Plowing was something the Triceratops was perfectly willing to do, because the plow weighed almost nothing as far as he was concerned. To him, plowing was little more than an excuse to simply walk back and forth in the fields. It was almost a summary of life in general, as far as he was concerned.

But today, Dismo seemed to be dragging.

"Dismo," called Eric after a time. "You know, we don't have to finish all this today. I have no problem with you stopping early for once."

"It makes no difference to me," Dismo replied, but Eric had known Dismo long enough to know that particular tone of voice. Dismo would be grateful for the break; it just wasn't in his personality to admit it. "If *you*, on the other hand, are tired…"

"Oh, I am," Eric said quickly, stepping off the plow and taking care to drag his feet to feign fatigue. "I'm exhausted."

"Well, we shall stop for you, then," said Dismo.

The only ones who seemed to be enjoying the weather were the insects, who were swarming thickly. Eric brushed some of them away in irritation and then said, "Let's head back to the barn. Call it a—*ow!*" Suddenly, he smacked his left arm with his palm.

"Call it an *ow?*" Dismo said, making no effort to hide his confusion. "What is an *ow?*"

Eric didn't answer. He was too busy wiping the mess away from his arm.

"Look at this!" Eric said in annoyance, holding his arm up in front of Dismo's face.

"*That* is an ow? I thought you called that an arm."

"Yes, of course it's an arm. But it's an arm decorated with a mess because this stupid insect bit me. I'm the last one he'll ever bite, though."

That much was certainly true. The insect, looking vaguely similar to a mosquito, had moved slowly. When it had landed on Eric's arm, it was apparently engorged with blood from something else. That hadn't stopped the bug from trying to tap into his veins as well. It was already under way when the stinging sensation on Eric's arm had alerted him to the tiny intruder. He had done a fairly thorough job of smashing the bug flat, and his arm now had a decent-sized patch of blood on it. He didn't know whether it was his, the insect's, or the blood of whomever else the insect had been feeding on before it had gotten to him. Perhaps it was all three.

Well, whatever it was, thought Eric, it was quickly becoming a forgotten problem. The stinging sensation was already subsiding. Rubbing his arm, he said, "What would you say to a game of Triassic once we get back?"

"Perhaps," Dismo said, "you might want to spend some time with Gwen. You do not have much opportunity to do so."

"Gwen?" Eric seemed puzzled by the suggestion. "Why would she want to spend time with me? She's a girl. She'd much rather spend time with girls her own age."

"He never wants to spend any time with me," Gwen complained to Cayley.

The girls were at the house, and Gwen was preparing a simple lunch for the two of them. Cayley had come to visit, and Gwen was happy for the company, particularly since she spent much of the day simply hanging around the house, doing chores, and keeping the home fires burning. Gwen did not consider it a very interesting existence, mostly because she felt she could be doing so much more.

"Why can't I be out in the fields with him?" she demanded of Cayley.

Cayley looked at her as if she were out of her mind. "In case you haven't noticed, it's sweltering outside. It's much cooler in here. You should consider yourself lucky."

"I don't feel lucky," Gwen said sourly. "I feel like there's so much more I could be doing. That I *should* be doing." Gwen removed one of her special soups from the fire and ladled it out into bowls for herself and Cayley. Then she sat down opposite her friend. "It's a world of possibilities out there, and Dad won't open his eyes to—"

The door abruptly thudded inward, causing both Gwen and Cayley to jump. Eric was standing at the door, and Dismo could be seen standing not too far off. Eric was scratching his arm absently, and there was a thick sheen of sweat on his forehead, which was not surprising considering the heat. Still, something about him seemed not quite right.

"Dad?" Gwen looked questioningly at him.

His gaze took in the entirety of the room. "Did you make anything for me?" he demanded.

"N-no," she said. There was something in his look, in the tone of his voice, that she really didn't like. "No, I didn't."

"Why not?"

"Because...because you never have lunch at this time. You usually just eat some fruit out in the field. You don't like to stop working if—"

"Did you see what it's like out today?" he demanded. "Are you being critical of me just because I felt like taking a little time off?"

"Mr. Corey," Cayley said quickly, "you can have mine. I wasn't really hungry."

Cayley pushed the soup toward him.

To the girls' utter shock, he clumsily knocked the bowl over, sending the contents splattering. Only Cayley's quick reflexes prevented her from getting soaked as she jumped out of the way just in time.

"Dad! What's wrong with you?" demanded Gwen.

He shook his head and rubbed his eyes. "Nothing. Nothing is wrong with me," he mumbled. "Is that understood?" When she didn't answer fast enough, he raised his voice and repeated, "Is that understood!"

Gwen's cheeks began to flush. She felt utterly mortified being scolded in front of her friend. She tried to say something, but she felt as if there were no breath in her lungs. Without a word, Gwen ran from the house. An instant later, Cayley was following, trying to keep up with her.

After the girls had gone, Gwen's father looked around the now empty home and felt a distant pounding in his head. What in the world had just happened? He wasn't at all sure. He'd felt fine only a few minutes ago, but something had put him in an incredibly foul mood. And his arm wouldn't stop itching.

Suddenly, Eric was starting to feel very tired. He decided that perhaps a nap would suit him better. Yes, a quick nap, that's all it would take, and he'd feel as good as new.

CHAPTER 5

Booj sat at the edge of the small pool where he always went when he felt unsure of what to do. He stared at his reflection.

The Velociraptor felt as if he had a great destiny in front of him, but he had no idea what it might be. He also knew that he didn't like Xin suggesting to him that he should leave. Booj hated being told what to do. That sort of thing really cracked his scales.

Then his thoughts wandered in another direction. He was reasonably sure that, whatever his destiny might be, it didn't lie with his fellow Velociraptors. Perhaps, all along, he had been trying to cause this moment to happen. Perhaps he had been creating the circumstances that would require him to leave so that he could discover where he was really meant to be.

"After all," Booj said aloud, "I am a Dinosaur of Destiny." He discovered that he liked the sound of that: Dinosaur of Destiny. It had something of a ring to it.

Booj also realized that he was much more comfortable with the explanation that he had just concocted. Xin wasn't in control of him. No, Xin was doing exactly what Booj wanted. Although he didn't realize it, Xin had played right into Booj's claws. This very notion caused Booj to laugh heartily and feel much better about the entire situation.

"That's that, then," Booj said confidently. "I don't have to let myself be bossed around by what other people want…but I certainly can't ignore what *I* want for myself!"

By the next morning, Booj was gone. The other Raptors immediately noticed, mainly because the village had suddenly become much, *much* quieter.

CHAPTER 6

"Gwen, come back!"

Gwen heard Cayley's call, but she would not slow down. She kept heading straight for the woods, even as her friend dashed after her.

When Gwen reached the woods, she plunged straight into them. The branches snagged and tore her clothes, but that didn't stop her. She was determined to leave the farmhouse behind. Her father had had no cause to scold her like that, no cause to criticize or berate her. She had no idea what had motivated him, nor did she care. All she wanted to be was gone, and that was exactly where she expected to be, very shortly.

What she did not expect was the ground to fall suddenly out from under her.

Boom! The branches and grass caved in beneath her feet. She barely had time to realize that there had been some sort of camouflage obscuring a leaf-lined hole in the ground, as if a trap had been laid. She had only a few seconds to prepare herself for what she anticipated would be a very deep plunge—and then her feet thudded on hard ground covered with thick leaves.

Gwen looked around in confusion to discover that she was standing in a pit that came only to the top of her head. The crumbling dirt around the edges would make it difficult for her to pull herself up, but certainly not impossible.

"Gwen!" She heard Cayley shouting her name. "Gwen!"

"Over here!" Gwen called and, moments later, Cayley was standing at the edge of the hole. Her friend looked down with an expression bordering on amusement.

"Building yourself a mini-swimming hole?" she asked innocently. "If you're planning to do any diving, you'll have to give it a bit more depth, don't you think?"

"Very funny."

"It is," Cayley said. "You should see your face."

"Are you going to help me out of here or not?" Gwen asked impatiently.

"I haven't made up my mind yet," Cayley teased.

"Cayley!"

"Who are you?" a voice interrupted.

The loud question startled both girls, and they turned their heads to find a young man standing nearby.

Tall and gawky, he regarded them with great suspicion. The stranger wore simple garments, except for his fine black waistcoat, which hung open. A large satchel was slung over his shoulder.

"Who are you?" he asked again, although this time he'd softened his voice slightly. "And what are you doing in my storage pit?"

"I didn't see it," said Gwen.

"That's because I covered it over," said the young man.

Gwen stared at him. "Uh, you know, that just may be why I *didn't see it.*"

"Oh. Right. I mean, sorry," said the stranger. "I didn't mean for you to fall in."

Gwen sighed. "Well what did you mean then? Why did you dig this trap in the first place?"

"It isn't a trap. It's a storage pit. To keep my scrolls. Or at least the ones I've finished studying. Only I haven't put any in there yet because I'm... well...still studying."

"Scrolls?" Cayley asked confused.

"Yes, scrolls. They're part of my Trial."

"Trial?" Gwen asked equally confused.

"I see this might take a while," the young man said. "The Trial is something that..."

His voice trailed off as he stared at Gwen.

"What is it?" asked Gwen suspiciously.

"I *know* you. You're the girl who lives down on that farm," the boy said. "I've seen you—and you've seen me."

"At night?" Slowly she was beginning to understand. "You were the one with the glowing eyes?"

He nodded.

"But how?" she asked.

The young man hunkered down next to the pit, reached into the satchel he had slung over his shoulder, and pulled out the oddest pair of goggles Gwen had ever seen. She knew that Skybax Riders sometimes wore such eye equipment, but she'd never seen gleaming red lenses before.

"Sunstone," he told her. "I found a way to slice them so thin that they're transparent. Then I polish them very thoroughly. They give me night vision to some degree—similar to how saurians see, I think."

"That's amazing," she said. "I'd admire them even more if I weren't stuck in this hole."

"Oh." This time he didn't bother to apologize, but instead grabbed her hand and pulled. He did so rather effortlessly, which was surprising given the general leanness of his body.

"So," Cayley said, "what we know about you so far is, you set traps that catch young girls and you've been spying on Gwen. Now, *why* is it that you were spying on her?"

"I...liked what I saw," he said with a shrug. "I don't get to see all that much here. I'm here as part of my Trial."

"What is this *Trial* thing? Are you in some sort of trouble or something?" Gwen asked.

At first, the stranger looked confused, but then he

seemed to understand and laughed heartily.

"No," he finally said. "Nothing like a criminal trial. It's—" Suddenly, he seemed to decide that he was getting ahead of himself. He stuck out a hand. "My name's Jason."

Gwen hesitated only a moment, and then she smiled slightly. Aside from his present odd endeavor, he seemed harmless enough. "My name's Gwen," she said. "This is Cayley."

Cayley still had suspicion in her eyes, but he seemed to accept it. "The Trial is...well, it's a family tradition. When you reach a certain age, as I have, you're expected to strike out on your own for six months."

"Six months?" Gwen was appalled. "That sounds kind of strange."

"Why? It simply helps prepare me for adulthood."

"If you say so."

"Come on." He turned and gestured for them to follow. Gwen started to, and Cayley said, "Are you sure that we should?"

Jason turned. "Come or don't come, it's up to you. On second thought, stay here." And with that he disappeared into the forest, which swallowed him up like a shadow.

"Oh, Gwen, we should get out of here," Cayley warned.

"But he seems nice."

"Nice! He caught you in a trap!"

"Well, not everyone is perfect."

Suddenly, Jason seemed to reappear out of thin air, his arms loaded with scrolls. He plopped down and held some of them up.

"The problem with adulthood," he said, "is that you're caught up in all the responsibilities of being an adult. When you're thirteen or fourteen, or thereabouts, you're starting the in-between stage. Not a child anymore but not an adult yet, either. The purpose of the Trial is to give you some time at the in-between stage, so you can think about what you're leaving behind and also what it is that's ahead. It's a time to figure out what you want to accomplish. You live on your own, fending for yourself, and you ponder stuff like this." He waved a couple of the scrolls around again in a manner indicating that the girls should take them.

Tentatively, they did, and unrolled them. "These are poems," Cayley said after a moment.

"And ballads," added Gwen.

"Yup. About history—in Dinotopia and elsewhere. About scientific principles and medicine. About philosophy and ethics. Goes on for scrolls and scrolls."

"What are you supposed to do with all this?" asked Gwen.

"Memorize it. Learn it, understand it, and take it in here—" He touched his chest.

"All of this? It looks like a lot," noted Cayley.

Once again, Jason laughed. "This? This is nothing. I built myself a tree house not far from here, and it's crammed with scrolls. This is barely a handful compared to everything that I have to study and learn. When I finally go home, my father will sit down and grill me. He'll make sure I've absorbed all of it, believe me."

"And if you haven't?" asked Cayley.

He looked at her as if to say that such a notion had never even occurred to him. "I will," he told her with quiet conviction. Then, more cheerfully, he added, "And why shouldn't I? I have no distractions. The purity of nature is all around me. I have all the time in the world. I couldn't be happier."

"Really." Gwen said it in a way that indicated she didn't quite believe him.

Jason paused a moment, and then sighed. "Well, the truth is, I'm kind of bored, actually. Even going a little crazy. I've been working and working, memorizing and memorizing. I feel like my head's getting completely filled up. What if there's no room for any more and I still have a hundred scrolls to go? What then?"

"Get another head?" suggested Cayley.

"All there is," he continued as if she hadn't spoken, "is nature and scrolls, scrolls and nature. My father told me that I would empty myself once I'm out and away from everything. I would become a vacant container that all the knowledge would flow into. But you know what? It's pretty dull being a container, when you get right down to it. I feel like I've got a lot of knowledge in my head, but nothing to do with it, you know? I guess I'm supposed to learn patience, too. But I don't know if I'm patient enough to learn patience."

This time it was Gwen who laughed, until she realized that he hadn't intended to make a joke. He looked at her as if he didn't understand what was so funny. "I'm sure you'll get it worked out, Jason," she said consolingly. "And you should at least be happy that you have a father who cares about your learning things. About being an asset to him and your family. If I never went back home, my father wouldn't even notice."

"I'm sorry that you feel that way," he said. "It'd be nice if you and your dad got along."

"He hates me. He yelled at me."

Jason shrugged once more. "My father yells at me. Doesn't mean that he doesn't love or care about me."

"It's different. You're a—well, it's just different. He was furious with me before, and I didn't do anything. Not a thing."

"Maybe he had something on his mind."

"Are you on his side?" demanded Gwen.

"I'm not on anybody's side," Jason said with a wry grin. "Look, you live your life as you think is right. Me, I'm just saying that you shouldn't toss aside your whole relationship because he got angry with you about something."

"I guess…"

*   *   *

Gwen talked with Jason for much of the day. Jason seemed pleased with the distraction, and Gwen was interested in getting a male point of view on her problems. Even Cayley warmed to him after a while when it became clear that he wasn't so very odd after all. In fact, Gwen guessed from the way Cayley never took her eyes off him that she was becoming a bit sweet on Jason. Gwen couldn't blame her. He was attractive-looking, in a gawky sort of way.

And then they heard something.

It was a call, a loud, high-pitched moan that sounded like a dinosaur roar, coming from some distance away.

Slowly Gwen rose to her feet, straining her ears. "Is that...?" She hesitated, and there it was again. "That's—that's coming from home. From the direction of the farm."

"Are you sure?" asked Cayley.

"That's Dismo! It has to be! Something's wrong!" Without hesitation, she ran. Cayley sprinted immediately after her, and, after only a moment's pause, Jason followed as well.

Gwen ran, heedless of anything in her path. She knew that if Dismo was sending out a call for help, then her father was the one in trouble. If Dismo himself had been hurt or injured, naturally her dad would be tending him. So the only conclusion to be drawn was that something was wrong with her father.

Suddenly, all the anger and cross words came back to haunt Gwen. What if something really bad had happened to him? What if his last memories of her were of anger? What if—?

Gwen forced herself to shake off those thoughts. She had to deal with one thing at a time. Maybe it was a misunderstanding. Maybe everything was going to be fine. Yes, it would be. It had to be.

She dashed out of the woods and across the open field. She spotted Dismo standing outside the farmhouse. The sun was already dropping low in the sky. "Dismo, what's happened?" she called, gasping for air. "Where's Dad?!"

"In there," said Dismo, with a wave of his horns. "We were playing a game of Triassic, but his mind seemed elsewhere. He said he wanted to lie down, but I just saw him through the window. He doesn't usually lie down on the floor, does he?"

Gwen burst through the door and then skidded to a halt, letting out a shriek of alarm.

Her father lay on the floor, arms outstretched. His breathing was shallow, and it was clear to her that he had simply collapsed. "Daddy!" she cried out, but he did not respond. Quickly, she went to him, trying to haul him up, and was horrified to feel his skin. He wasn't sweating but was hot to the touch, burning hot. Immediately, she knew this was fever. He was burning up from the inside.

Gwen heard the pounding of footsteps behind

41

her, and then Cayley and Jason were there. "Help me!" she called to them, and immediately they were next to her. Cayley grabbed Eric's left arm, Gwen his right, Jason his legs, and between the three of them they were able to haul him over to his bed and lay him down.

"He's feverish," said Jason.

"I know!" Gwen was frantic.

"Look at this!" Cayley said. She was standing next to his left arm, pointing to a swelling.

Gwen and Jason looked carefully at it. There was a large red rash radiating out from what appeared to be some sort of bite mark. It covered much of his upper arm.

"I don't like the looks of that," Jason said.

"Cayley, go into town," Gwen said urgently. "Get Doc Traptor. Hurry. Hurry!"

Cayley left at once. Gwen watched her go, then turned to see that Jason had placed his satchel on the table and was removing some of the contents.

Gwen looked on in confusion. There was an assortment of roots, herbs, and other things gathered from the forest. Jason pulled out a small wooden bowl and what appeared to be a rounded, spoon-like tool.

"What—what is that? What are you doing?" Gwen asked.

Jason pointed to the bowl and utensil. "A mortar and pestle," he said, then began measuring different herbs and roots into the mortar.

"I could use some water if you have any," he said.

"I have some in my container, but I'd rather save it."

Gwen quickly obeyed, running out to the trough with a large cup and filling it. She hurried back to discover that Jason had already thoroughly mashed the herbs and roots together using the thing he'd called a pestle.

"Excellent. Thank you," he said in a brisk, no-nonsense voice. He added a small amount of water and within moments had a paste-like substance.

He removed a dull knife from his satchel, took the mortar in one hand, and moved quickly over to Gwen's father. Using the knife, he carefully began to smooth the paste on the rash.

"What is that?" Gwen finally asked. "What are you doing?"

"It's something that helps fight infection. I'm hoping it will do some good," he told her.

"You always carry that around with you?"

"Of course," he said. "I'm on my own. If I injure myself, I have to be able to patch myself up no matter where I am."

Gwen saw her father's mouth start to move. "Daddy?" she whispered, and went to him. "Daddy? Can you hear me?"

"Thirs—thirsty," he managed to say.

"Yes, yes, I'll get you water."

"Don't just pour a cup of it down his throat," cautioned Jason. "He could gag or choke. Wet a cloth and have him suck the moisture out of it."

She did as Jason instructed, holding the cloth to her father's mouth. He didn't seem aware that she was doing it. He didn't seem aware of anything. She shook her head in worry, and glanced at Jason to see the same concern in his eyes.

And in a very low voice, so low that her father couldn't hear, she whispered to Jason, "Is he…is he going to die?"

"I don't know," Jason replied. "I just don't know."

CHAPTER 7

Dr. Traptor was actually two individuals whom the townspeople had come to refer to as one: a human and a dinosaur who had bonded into an inseparable team.

The human was Dr. Augustus Trapp. He was a fairly short gentleman, from Austria originally, with a thick, graying beard and a manner that indicated an almost infinite amount of patience.

The dinosaur was, essentially, his nurse and medical associate. Her name was Ulla, and she was a Megaraptor. Stretching twenty-three feet from nose tip to tail, Ulla was capable of covering a large distance very quickly. This was a great benefit to Dr. Trapp. When an emergency summoned him, he would simply leap onto Ulla's back and she would take him there, quick as the wind.

Ulla also assisted him in whatever needed doing— particularly surgery, where her razor-sharp claws were capable of creating incisions with beyond-human precision.

Consequently, the residents of Dinotopia had come to refer to Dr. Trapp and his Raptor associate by one name: Dr. Traptor. At first this annoyed Dr. Trapp a bit, since he thought he was being mocked, but eventually he came to understand that it was a term of affection. These days he even referred to himself and Ulla by that same name.

It took the doctor half an hour to reach the Corey farm: twenty minutes for a breathless Cayley to get to his office, and ten minutes for the speedy Raptor to transport Trapp and Cayley back. Without a word, the doctor began to examine his patient. He immediately noticed the salve on Eric's arm. "What is this?" he asked. "Who put this on him?"

"I did," Jason said.

The doctor studied it a moment, then nodded with thin-lipped approval. "Not bad, but I have to look at what's under it." He wiped it clean and studied the bite on the arm.

Then he touched Eric's throat on either side, just under his chin, and Gwen's father moaned in distant pain. The doctor proceeded to ask Gwen a series of questions regarding her father's health and assorted symptoms. And then he said, "The saurian. I want to see the saurian—the Trike that lives here."

Dismo had not wandered far away. His usual aloof air was gone now, and he appeared just as concerned about Eric as everyone else. The doctor proceeded to examine Dismo from one end to the other, with the aid of a large magnifying glass. Finally, somewhere around the area of Dismo's right hip, he let out a "Mm-hmm." Then he went back into the house, where Gwen and the others were waiting for him. Getting right to the heart of the matter, he said, "Your father is suffering from Zinix disease."

"What's Zinix disease?" she asked.

Before the doctor could reply, Jason spoke up. "I thought only dinosaurs could get that."

"You seem rather up to date on a variety of medical matters, lad," observed the doctor.

"I've read a lot. Especially lately."

"Mmm. Yes, well, Zinix *is* primarily a dinosaur illness, particularly carried in older saurians. A viral infection that, to saurians, is relatively harmless. Causes, at most, mild joint discomfort. That's about it. In humans, however, it's far more destructive. Transmission is not a simple thing, though. It usually requires some sort of exchange of fluids. Ingestion, for instance, or saliva transmitted via mouth."

"You mean..." Gwen looked at her father in astonishment. "You mean Dad was *kissing* Dismo? On the beak?"

"*Ewww,*" Cayley said.

Despite the seriousness of the situation, it took the doctor a moment to fight down an impulse to laugh. "No," he said. "That's rather unlikely. No, it was this," and he pointed to the inflammation on her father's arm. "An insect bite, most probably by the bit-

47

ing midge known as the Culicoide. There was a similar bite on Dismo."

"I didn't feel it," Dismo rumbled, standing near the door.

"You probably wouldn't. Not with the thickness of your skin. The insect drained blood from you, Dismo, and then moved on to Mr. Corey here. When he crushed the insect, your blood mixed with his own. Because it was injected directly into his bloodstream, the disease has spread through him very quickly."

"So how do we cure it?" asked Gwen. "What kind of medicine do you have?"

The doctor glanced at Ulla, who was sadly shaking her head. Then he stepped closer to Gwen. "I regret to tell you this, my dear, but there isn't any," he said in his gentle Austrian accent.

"Well, where do we get it, then, if we don't have any here?"

Although Dr. Traptor was a small man, his hands were rather large, and he took her hands in his. "There is no cure, Gwen," he said slowly and carefully. "The saurians have never developed one because the ailment is so minor to them, and transmission into human hosts is so rare that there's never been any real research into it. There's nothing we can do except make him comfortable and keep him away from any form of human contact. Zinix disease is incredibly contagious, Gwen. He cannot come in physical contact with any human. If he does, it could be deadly."

"What about that herb—Trilobur? Shouldn't that take care of it? Heal him?" Jason suggested.

Dr. Traptor shook his head. "As a preventative, it might have been of some help. Maybe if he'd realized immediately and taken some within, say, a few minutes of contact. Taking it now that the infection has already set in won't help." Then Dr. Traptor took a moment to clear his throat. He addressed Gwen with a look of sympathetic affection. "As harmless as it is in saurians, it's extremely vicious in humans. Trilobur won't even begin to slow it down at this stage."

"You can't mean it." Gwen started to tremble, although whether it was with fear or anger, she couldn't be certain. "We can't just...just sit around and wait for him to die! We have to do something! Something!"

"We can treat his symptoms—the fever, the delirium, the sweating—but that's all we'll be able to do. The infection will continue to spread through his body. I have no medicine that can counter it. I'm sorry, Gwen. I'm so sorry."

"I don't want your 'sorry'! I want my father!"

She began to cry. Cayley held Gwen close as she sobbed on her friend's shoulder. Her father didn't even stir. He probably couldn't hear her at all.

CHAPTER 8

Several hours later, darkness had settled over the farm.

Cayley was preparing dinner.

The doctor, who had other patients, promised that he would stop back frequently to look in on Eric.

And Jason...

Jason had disappeared.

Gwen wasn't certain when he'd left. He'd slipped away without a word. It made her wonder what kind of a person he was. Instead of sticking close in her time of need, he had abandoned her.

Her father lay on his bed, sleeping. Every so often he would moan softly or shudder. At those times she and Cayley would tend to him as best they could. They were very careful not to directly touch their skin to his, as Doctor Traptor had instructed. Except for an overwhelming sense of helplessness and frustration, Gwen felt numb.

A tapping began on the roof, then increased in strength. Gwen realized it was starting to rain. A crack of thunder told her that it was going to be a heavy storm. She drew the blanket up to her father's chin while Cayley stoked the fire to make sure that the winds, which were starting to whistle down the chimney, didn't extinguish it.

Gwen sat at the foot of her father's bed and watched the unsteady rising and falling of his chest. "Cayley, his life is slipping away. I can't believe it."

"I know," Cayley told her.

Suddenly, a deafening thunderclap boomed so loudly that the girls put their hands over their ears. At that precise moment, the door to the farmhouse burst open. A figure towered in the doorway as lightning lit up the area and thunder erupted once more. The effect was so startling that both girls let out an involuntary scream.

"Sorry! Sorry!" came a now familiar voice, and the girls immediately realized it was Jason. His fine black waistcoat was buttoned, a brown cloak hung across his shoulders, and his hair was soaking wet from the rain.

"That entrance was much more dramatic than I'd intended," Jason said. Then he turned and managed to shove the door shut against the rushing wind. "I really didn't mean to startle you."

"Well, you did," Gwen said coolly. "Where did you go?"

"Back to my place. For this." He shrugged off his wet cloak and pulled out a rolled-up scroll. Quickly, he opened it. "Took me a while to find it, but I knew

I'd seen something about it. It might give your father a chance."

"What are you talking about?" demanded Cayley. "The doctor said her father didn't have a—"

"Dr. Traptor is a great doctor," said Jason readily. "But he's not a historian."

"Historian?" Gwen seemed as confused as Cayley. "I don't—"

"My family has history, Gwen. And my family *is* history. We go back, way back." He paused for dramatic effect. "We're an early family."

"You mean your family goes all the way back to—"

"To some of the earliest humans shipwrecked on Dinotopia," Jason finished for her. "And my family recorded much of their history. That's part of what we've tried to preserve through all our scrolls. That's part of the Trial. So each new generation will learn the family history—along with a number of other things, of course."

"And? What does this have to do with my father?"

Jason leaned forward, his knuckles resting on the table as he smoothed out the scroll. Then he answered Gwen with one word: "Odon."

Cayley and Gwen exchanged looks. "I'm sorry?" Gwen shook her head. "Is that supposed to mean something?"

"Odon," Jason explained, "is a legendary healer. The greatest in the history of Dinotopia. Next to him,

52

Doc Traptor—even with all his skill and experience—is a novice."

"Odon...is he a human? Or a saurian?"

"Saurian. Don't know what type. The scrolls don't say. What they do say is that he could cure anything. Or at least almost anything. But he disappeared long ago. Left Dinotopian society."

"Well, that's just terrific," Gwen said. "If he vanished long ago, how can we expect him to still be alive?"

"If he kept eating the herb for long life, he likely is."

"But you said he vanished," Cayley said. "Why? If he was so wonderful, why did he leave?"

Jason took a deep breath. "Odon believed that the teaming of humans and dinosaurs was against nature."

"What?" Gwen couldn't believe what she was hearing, nor could Cayley. In the Dinotopia that they had grown up in, the human-saurian alliance was one of the cornerstones of life. "How could he have believed that? It doesn't seem possible."

"It was very possible. It all stems from the earliest times—and events of which many modern-day Dinotopians are not even aware." He cleared his throat. "Have you got anything to drink around here? My throat's parched."

Gwen rose to get him a cup of water. He took it gratefully and sat.

"There was a time…long, long ago," Jason continued slowly. "A time when the very first humans arrived on Dinotopia and didn't understand."

"What do you mean?" Gwen asked. "Didn't understand what?"

"Didn't understand that saurians and humans could live in harmony. There are stories about terrible human behavior…stories that are the saurian equivalent of the bogeyman. Stories that some saurians, like Odon, heard when he was just a hatchling."

"What kind of stories?"

Thunder rumbled overhead as if to underscore his reply: "Hunters."

"Hunters?" The girls weren't following. "What do you mean, hunters?"

"There are stories of humans who hunted the dinosaurs. Hunted them with fearsome weapons, so that they could collect them, make trophies of them, and—"

"Oh, this is barbaric!" exclaimed Gwen. "Humans could never have hunted the dinosaurs! They are our friends, our companions! And we are theirs!"

"I know it's unthinkable to you, but these tales are like ghost stories you might hear around a campfire. They're likely not true, but in the back of your mind, the stories haunt you. And, well, long ago some older saurians, after hearing such stories as hatchlings, harbored a belief that humans might one day hunt them again."

"I've heard enough of this!" Gwen declared loudly. "All this silliness—it has absolutely nothing to do with my father! None of it is going to make the slightest bit of difference in curing him!"

"It actually has everything to do with it, if you'll just let me finish," Jason told her with a slightly scolding tone in his voice.

"Fine, fine," she said.

Jason pulled out another scroll and unrolled it on the table. "There are some accounts that say when humans first began arriving in Dinotopia, ages ago, there was resistance. Some humans were hostile. And some saurians did not trust them. The mistrust of humans was further heightened by odd human behavior—"

"Odd behavior? Like what?" asked Cayley.

"Oh, like, for instance, the human penchant for arboreal life. One of my scrolls says that the earliest humans were frightened and suspicious of the saurians, and sought refuge in trees. Arboreal habitats were completely unknown to dinosaurs, and for some of them, it was quite strange and disturbing.

"As time went by, the humans and dinosaurs befriended each other. They gradually built Dinotopia up into what it is today, and many of those old fears simply vanished. Now the threat of the hunters has faded into obscurity. But the Maze remains."

"The what?"

"The Maze, Gwen," he told her. "In this region of Dinotopia, the fear of hostile newcomers became

quite strong at one time. So the mutual decision was made, between a small group of saurian and human families, that a sort of fortress might be appropriate in the case of such hostile newcomers. They constructed a maze, a place of safety where they could secure themselves if invaders came to Dinotopia. It was one of the earliest—perhaps *the* earliest—cooperative efforts between humans and dinosaurs. It's huge, built underground, with only a handful of secret entrances."

"Where are these entrances?'" asked Gwen.

"No one knows for sure. Otherwise they wouldn't be secret, now would they?"

Gwen didn't particularly care for Jason's slightly patronizing tone of voice, but she let it slide.

"The Maze," continued Jason, "is supposedly filled with deathtraps. Any dinosaurs who desired to take refuge there would have been able to find their way through. They knew ahead of time all the right twists and turns they had to take to avoid the hazards. Humans, likewise—those allied with the saurians—would know the safe ways to pass through the Maze.

"Unfortunately, none of these 'safe' instructions exist in this day and age. They were passed down orally because the dinosaurs of the time didn't want to take a chance that documents might be found that would safely guide any hostile humans—any 'hunters'— through. However, as time passed, the bond between saurians and humans grew, and the Maze seemed little more than a relic of a paranoid time long past."

"I still don't understand how this will help my father," murmured Gwen. But then suddenly it dawned on her. "Wait a minute," she said. "You're about to tell me that *Odon* is hiding down in this Maze somewhere."

"That's right," Jason affirmed. "According to my scroll, Odon was wary of humans and came to believe that humans and dinosaurs should not work together. He was a pure naturalist and claimed that nature had never intended for saurian and man to coexist. After all, mankind didn't come along until thousands of millennia after the Mesozoic era. Odon believed that if humans and saurians were meant to coexist, they would have in the first place. The scroll also explains that some terrible event occurred while Odon was working as a healer."

"What event?" Gwen asked.

"The scroll doesn't say. What it does say, however, is that this event made Odon come to the conclusion that humans and saurians should not live together. Odon was believed to have taken permanent refuge in the Maze. There he vowed to live until he saw some sort of proof that the human-saurian symbiosis could work."

"And where would this Maze be?"

"Not sure."

"You're not sure!" cried an exasperated Cayley. She turned to Gwen. "He doesn't know where the secret entrances are because they're secret, and now he doesn't even know where the Maze itself is so that we can look!"

"I said I wasn't sure," Jason said calmly. "I have some good ideas, though. The scrolls give general indications."

"Jason, this is asking a lot from me," Gwen told him. "You're asking me to accept, on faith, this healer's existence. That he's still even alive. You're asking me to accept that he might know of some cure for my father. You're asking me to help find a Maze, the whereabouts of which we don't know, so that you can navigate the Maze, the design of which you don't know, in order to contact a healer who we don't know is alive, or even there, in order to save my father from a disease that we're told is incurable."

"Wait, wait…back up," Jason said, suddenly looking nervous. "What do you mean, so that I can navigate the Maze? I came here to give you a hope, a direction in which you could go if you were so inclined. But I'm not going. No, no. I'll give you as much information as I can, but I have my Trial to finish."

"Jason, I can't do it without you! I probably can't even do it *with* you!"

"Well, that's your choice, Gwen. Here." He gave the scrolls to her. "Do what you wish with them."

Gwen stared at the scrolls as Jason turned to go. She had to stop him, had to think of something to say to change his mind. "You…you coward."

He stared at her. "What?"

"You heard me." She drew herself up. "You coward."

"I'm no coward," he said hotly. "You have no right to call me that."

Cayley's gaze shifted from one to the other, back and forth.

"No, I don't," agreed Gwen readily. "No reason except one. How do you know that *this* isn't your true Trial?"

"What?"

"This! Helping me find Odon. Look, you've got all this knowledge gathered in your head. Well, you know what? It's gathering dust unless you go out and do something with it. You need a quest."

"A quest?" echoed Cayley. "What's a quest?"

"A journey," Jason told her without glancing in her direction. He hadn't removed his gaze from Gwen. "A voyage to get out and do something, try for something ambitious. I've been reading scrolls like those, adventures and stories of heroes. Amazing stories. People who took chances and did great things. People who helped whenever they could simply because it was the right thing to do."

There was a long moment of silence, broken only by a few drops of rain on the rooftop. The thunder had moved off, and it sounded as if the rain was nearly done as well.

"Gwen," said Jason finally, "you realize that there's almost no chance—"

"But *almost* no chance is a lot better than absolutely no chance."

Jason sighed.

"Don't you see?" Gwen told him. "You're too satisfied with simply reading *about* history. Maybe you should be brave enough to try making some. Now, wouldn't that be a great thing to record in a scroll?"

Jason stared at her a long moment, then abruptly turned and walked out.

Gwen looked at her father as the door closed behind Jason. She stood there for a long moment, watching his labored breathing. She thought of all the angry thoughts she had had about him, everything that she'd wanted from the relationship that now would never be.

"Cayley," she suddenly said with new conviction in her voice, "I need you to watch my dad. To take care of him."

"Okay. For how long?" Then her voice trailed off as she realized. "You're going off on this crazy quest, aren't you? All by yourself."

Gwen was busy getting a cloak to wrap around herself. "It's that or nothing. And if it's the only choice I have, I'll go with it."

"Gwen!"

"What?" Gwen asked as she quickly shoved a few belongings into a pack, including the scrolls that Jason had handed her.

Cayley's voice softened. "I'll stay with him. For

however long it takes, I'll stay with him. You do what you have to do."

She held out a hand, and Gwen gripped it firmly. And then, since that didn't seem sufficient somehow, Gwen reached out and embraced her. Cayley held her tightly and whispered in her ear, "Come back in one piece. Your getting killed isn't going to do anything to help your father, and it'll just annoy me."

"Don't worry about that. I'm coming back. I'm too stubborn to die. And you remember, *keep him away from everyone*. Remember what Traptor said—no human contact."

"Don't worry, Gwen," Cayley responded. "I'll make sure."

Gwen went quickly to the door and yanked it open—and almost collided with Jason, who was standing just outside.

Despite the seriousness of the situation, she couldn't keep an amused smile from breaking across her face.

"Going somewhere without me?" he asked.

"I knew you'd come," Gwen replied. "Do you want to come in and we'll wait for morning?"

He gestured toward her father. "Do you think he can afford the time?"

The truth of the words hit her like a hammer blow as she realized just how little time they had. "You're right. We go now. I'll get a lantern."

"Big, clunky, and unreliable. Here. I always keep

an extra pair of these with me. You can use them."

He extended a pair of the goggles that she had seen him wearing earlier—the ones that gave him night vision. She slid them on her face and gasped as the world around her came alive. It was still dark, even through the glasses, but she was amazed by how much she could now see.

He had already slid on the other pair. "Ready to go," he said. "You?"

"Absolutely."

"And I'm not a coward."

"Absolutely not."

CHAPTER 9

The sun had risen on such a glorious day that some-how Gwen found it difficult to believe that she was on a quest to save her father's life. Instead, it seemed a day that called for laziness, for taking it easy. It was, in short, too pretty a day for life-and-death situations.

Unfortunately, that was exactly what Gwen had in front of her.

Jason set a fairly brisk pace, and the two walked the whole day before they felt exhaustion weighing them down. Deciding to stop for the night, they climbed a large tree with broad and sturdy branches. Gwen slept fitfully, dreams of mazes and traps flitting through her brain.

When she awoke the next morning, she discovered Jason staring at her, and he smiled upon seeing that she was awake again. The sun was beginning to rise as they set out.

The way ahead of them was more rigorous. Jason started up a rocky and fairly narrow path. Gwen didn't exactly like the looks of it, but she followed gamely, determined that there was nothing Jason could do that she wasn't capable of as well.

They climbed up and up as the terrain got more mountainous. Below her she could hear the sound of rushing water. It was very likely a tributary that fed into the Polongo River, and from the sound of it, the water was moving quickly.

"So where are we going?" she asked. "You seem to be heading in a definite direction, and you've acted so certain of yourself that I didn't want to say anything. But now that we're in the middle of making a kind of dangerous climb, it'd be nice to have some idea of where we're going."

"We're heading to the Foothills."

The Foothills were smaller mountains at the base of the range that had Volcaneum at its southern tip.

"Why the Foothills?" she asked.

"Because in one of the ballads that actually talks about the Maze, there are some lines that make me think that's where we can find an entrance."

He recited from memory:

> *You must go in striding to the place of hiding,*
> *From the mountain of heated depth,*
> *With feet and saurian's breath lit on high,*
> *Do hide the way inside.*

"What does all that mean?" asked Gwen. She noticed the trail they were following was narrowing even more. Now it was barely wider than a ledge that clung to the side of the hills they were climbing. Gwen had never been terribly comfortable with heights, but she wasn't going to admit that to Jason if she could help it. She forced herself to keep walking as if nothing was wrong.

"Well," said Jason easily, "'the place of hiding'" refers to the Maze itself. 'Go in striding' means that you have to walk there, which indicates that it's somewhere so narrow that traveling by Skybax wouldn't be practical. 'The mountain of heated depth' has got to refer to Volcaneum. And since there's the mention of feet, I'm taking that to mean the Foothills."

"And 'saurian's breath'?"

"Not sure about that one," Jason admitted. "I'm taking that to mean that because it's a long walk, you might be out of breath. But I'm having us take this shortcut through the Outer Ridge Crossing, which leads into the Foothills. Saurians wouldn't usually come this way because the passages are so narrow. So we're saving some time, at least."

"Jason."

"Yeah?" He turned to face her.

"Thank you," Gwen said sincerely. "For caring about my dad. For doing this."

"It's okay," he said. "It's nothing we even have to discuss."

"I know. But I hadn't really said thank you, and I felt that I should."

"It's not a problem. Watch your step there."

A piece of the ridge suddenly gave way underneath Gwen's feet.

She let out a shriek, pinwheeling her arms as she tried to throw herself against the mountainside. For the briefest of moments she felt herself starting to fall, and suddenly Jason's hand grabbed her by the wrist. He yanked her as hard and desperately as he could. The toes of her boots snagged the ledge section where Jason was standing, and he braced her against it, giving her a moment to catch her breath.

"Are you okay?" he asked.

"Y-yes," she managed to get out. "That was a lot closer than I would have wanted."

"You're going to be okay," he assured her, patting her confidently on the shoulder. "I won't let anything happen to you."

"That's—that's very good to know."

"Now just watch me, and go where I go."

He took a confident step forward—and the ridge went completely out from under him!

He didn't have time to jump, didn't have time to lunge to safety. All he could do was fall.

Instinctively, Gwen reached out to save him, grabbing him by the forearm. It was an extremely brave thing for her to do, but between his weight, the angle, and the pull of gravity, it was physically impossible for her to prevent his fall. Instead, Gwen was hauled completely off-balance, and she toppled forward as Jason yelled, "Don't!"

But it was too late. They both fell toward the river below. Jason reached the water first and hit with a loud splash. A second later, Gwen landed beside him. As she went under, water filled her nostrils. She fought desperately to regain the surface.

Kicking fiercely, she shoved herself upward. Finally, her face broke the surface. The water was flowing quickly. White-crested chop was shoving her along. She gasped, sucking in lungfuls of air, but the current pulled her under again. This time, she managed to get her head above water much faster, but she was still helpless to overcome the relentless pull of the river.

Something banged into her. For a moment, she thought it was a large rock, but then Jason's head bobbed to the surface. Fortunately enough, the rest of him was still attached to the head.

"Hold on!" he shouted, although there was nothing she could have possibly held on to. The shoreline was not that far away, but even though Gwen was a strong swimmer, she couldn't begin to make headway against the force of the river. They were helpless.

And then, Gwen was able to make out something else. It seemed as if the water was getting louder and moving faster. In fact, it sounded as if it was falling.

A waterfall, Gwen abruptly realized. *We're heading for a waterfall!*

For the past few days, Booj the Velociraptor had been heading into the heart of Dinotopia to seek his destiny. However, it seemed to Booj that his destiny didn't seem particularly anxious to find him.

As he walked away from his village, he dwelled on everything that Xin had said to him. He realized what had stung him the most was being told he didn't care about anyone or anything except himself. What an awful thing to accuse someone of.

Booj knew that he wasn't selfish. He knew that he considered others. However, as he searched back through his memory, he realized that most of his activities really had been designed to provide interest and entertainment for himself alone.

Booj had always felt himself to be something of a loner by nature. He had never felt especially attached to anyone and had never felt that anyone else particularly liked him.

It was just the circumstances, that's all, he told himself. It was the circumstances that had given the appearance that he was someone who was selfish. He knew that, given the opportunity, he could be as unselfish and giving as anyone else. That's what he told himself, anyway.

"That's better!" he said out loud as he came upon a river. It was a wide river, and the current was moving very quickly. He was at the base of a small mountain range, and there were some rocky extensions over his head, which provided him comfortable shade as he pondered his situation. He could hear the rushing of a waterfall a short distance away.

"If I had the chance, not only could I show that I care about others, but I could accomplish some of the greatest things in the history of Dinotopia! I know I could. Doesn't matter how much of a leap in the dark is involved; I'd be up to any challenge! I would!"

And then he heard a shriek.

Booj's head whipped around in confusion. The voice had been a human's. A female, he thought, by the sound of it. But then he heard another cry, and this one sounded a little deeper. Another human, possibly, and male.

He craned his neck, looking down the river in the direction that he'd thought he'd heard the shouts. Sure enough, he saw them coming, struggling and fighting the current mightily, but to no avail. Within seconds, Booj realized they were going to be swept right past him and over the falls that thundered in the distance.

And he had absolutely no idea what to do about it.

Nothing was going Gwen's way. She had steeled herself for the very real possibility that she might die in the Maze in a futile effort to find a healer who might not even be alive anymore. But somehow it had never occurred to her that she might meet her end without even having gotten close to the Maze at all!

It all seemed a great, terrible waste.

And then, just when she was sure that nothing could get worse, she heard a low rumble. It was the sound of rocks falling. *It's not enough that we're going to drown, we have to be knocked unconscious as well!*

Then she realized that the rockfall was in front of them. And she saw something else then that truly astounded her. The mini-avalanche was being caused by a dinosaur.

It appeared to be a Velociraptor. A rather large one, too. He was standing at the shoreline and had torn at the rocky extensions above him with his claws. He had managed to create a rockslide right at the water's edge by targeting a particularly precarious area and knocking the supports out from under it. The debris tumbled into the water and created a makeshift jetty of rock stretching several feet away from the shore.

The Raptor quickly hopped from one large rock to the next, never taking his eyes off the oncoming humans. His tail twitched nervously, and he looked with apprehension at his claws. Gwen knew that if the Raptor snatched at them too forcefully, he might accidentally claw them up. His claws, after all, were designed to be lethal, not life-saving. Dexterity was not a major consideration for an animal evolved to feed itself by rending and tearing.

But Gwen knew it was the only hope they had. He could have tried to let them grab at his tail, but the water was moving them too quickly and their hands were very slippery. And if they went past him at this point, there was no way he was going to be able to save them.

She watched the saurian balance himself at the end of his makeshift jetty. When they hurtled by him, he suddenly lunged to the side. Rocks shifted beneath his clawed feet, but the Raptor managed to keep from tumbling into the river along with them. Instead, he reached out and cleanly snatched one of their hands in each of his claws. He closed his talons around them as delicately as he could and hauled them toward safety. With their free hands, Gwen and Jason grabbed on to the rocks.

"You can make it! Come on!" squawked the Raptor as they hauled themselves toward shore. Within a few minutes, they had finally reached solid ground, where they flopped down, panting in exhaustion.

"Are you all right?" asked the Raptor.

"Fine. We're fine," grunted Jason. "Thanks for your help."

"Oh, you're quite welcome," the Raptor said, then suddenly paused in surprise. "Wait! You understand what I'm saying? You speak my language!"

"I know. My accent isn't great."

"It's terrible, actually, but I was trying to be polite."

Jason ignored the comment. "I've taken extensive lessons in the various saurian languages."

"What about her?" The Raptor turned his gaze to

Gwen, who was coughing up water. "Does she understand? Will she be all right?"

When she managed to pull herself together, Gwen managed to say, "I'm not as—as fluent as Jason here. A Triceratops I know taught me a bit, though. And I'll—I'll live. Thanks to you," she said, looking at the dinosaur in relief. "What's your name?"

He told them.

Gwen seemed mildly surprised. "Butch?" She turned to Jason. "Did he say his name was Butch?"

"I think so. Glad to meet you, Butch!" said Jason.

"No!" the dinosaur squawked. "Booj."

"Oh!" said Jason and Gwen at once.

"You're nowhere near a human village," Booj said. "Why are you here?"

Gwen quickly told him the nature of their expedition. Booj listened to it thoughtfully, nodding his head. "I've never heard of that ballad or the Maze," he said finally, "but I've heard of Odon. Borders on the mythic. They say that he disappeared long ago, after the plague."

"Plague?" For once, Jason looked surprised. "What plague? I don't know anything about a plague."

"Could it be in one of the scrolls you haven't gotten to yet?" suggested Gwen.

"I—I guess so. Still, I don't remember my parents ever mentioning it."

Booj shrugged. "My village has a fairly clear recollection of it. A lot of dinosaurs died during it. A lot.

Perhaps Odon did as well, now that I think about it."

"If he's alive and we can find him," Gwen asked, choosing to concentrate on the positive, "do you think he can help us?"

"I don't know," said Booj. "But I will tell you one thing: if anyone in Dinotopia can help you, it's him."

"We've got to reach the Foothills," said Jason. "Is there a better way to go than the long way around? The ridges seem a little"—he glanced upward worriedly—"treacherous."

"There *are* other ways," said Booj. "But you don't want to go there."

"You can't talk us out of this, Booj," Jason said. "We're determined to go to the Foothills."

"The Foothills. Are you sure?" asked Booj.

"Positive," Gwen affirmed.

"All right," Booj said slowly. He pointed. "If you follow the river's edge about two miles, there's a pass. It's somewhat rugged, but it won't fall apart on you. If you've got spirit, determination, and drive, you should be able to cover the distance in about a day. That'll put you at the base of the Foothills."

"Thank you," said Gwen. "We really appreciate this."

"Absolutely, yes," echoed Jason.

"You're quite welcome," said Booj warmly.

He leaned back and watched them move off in the direction that he'd sent them. He waited until they'd gotten about a hundred feet, and then called,

"By the way, about the Maze…"

"What about the Maze?" asked Gwen as she turned around.

Booj tilted his head, gesturing behind himself. "It's in the other direction."

They walked back to him, looking confused. "What do you mean, it's in the other direction?" asked Jason.

"I think the sentence speaks for itself, don't you?"

"But you said the Foothills were that way!" Gwen cried.

"They are," said Booj. "But the Maze is the other way."

"I don't understand!" said Gwen. "You told us you never heard of the Maze!"

"No, I haven't. But that poem segment you told me—how does it go again?"

"'You must go in striding to the place of hiding,'" quoted Jason. "'From the mountain of heated depth, with feet and saurian's breath lit on high, do hide the way inside.'"

"It's not the Foothills," Booj said. "That much I'm certain of."

"Well, do you know what it is?" asked Jason anxiously.

"I believe so, yes," said Booj. He tilted his head slightly, and there was something in his eyes that signaled amusement. "But you seemed so determined about the Foothills, I hated to get in your way."

"What makes you think we're wrong?" Jason asked.

"Because I know where the dinosaur feet are," Booj said with confidence. "You can come along, and I can show you."

"You'd help us?" Gwen asked.

"Certainly. My pleasure. And," he added slowly, "you might wish to return a favor for a favor?"

"What did you have in mind?" Jason asked.

Booj looked at Jason thoughtfully. "I've always liked being noticed. Standing out, you know? And I think you can help me in that regard."

"How?"

Booj paused a moment, and then tapped Jason's shoulder. "That," he said, "is a very, very fine waist-coat. Would you happen to know what size it is?"

CHAPTER 10

In his mind, Eric Corey could see his daughter's face.

Gwen became a haze of images as different moments of her life came tumbling, one after another. She seemed to grow up overnight, developing from an infant incapable of lifting her head into a young lady on the brink of adulthood, moving with grace and elegance.

And now Eric could see something in her eyes that he never had seen before. It was—it was accusation. Yes, that was it. A look of accusation. Why hadn't he noticed it before?

All the times she tried to speak to him about the things on her mind, and he never listened. All the times he brushed her aside and found something else to do. All the times he was too busy or too involved. All the times she reached out to him, but he wouldn't have anything to do with her.

Why? Why did all of this happen?

As Eric floated in a haze between consciousness and unconsciousness, many aspects of his life seemed to crystallize. He saw patterns he had never noticed before, found himself analyzing behavior he hadn't even been aware of.

There were so many challenges in raising a daughter alone while trying to run a farm. She asked about so many things, and he felt he should have all the answers because he was the only person around for her.

Too often he would turn away before the conversation could possibly lead to something beyond what he could handle. He felt that if he didn't have the answers Gwen was seeking, he would be letting her down. However, it now appeared that turning away had let her down even more.

Eric knew he should have been there for her, putting her first, placing consideration for her above his own problems. He was the adult, after all, and he owed it to her to behave as an adult.

It wasn't too late. Eric knew that with startling clarity. It wasn't too late to begin making things up to his daughter. He'd make her realize that he *did* love her and care for her. He was determined to try and make things right between them.

Eric tried to reach out a hand to Gwen. He could see her standing there, just out of reach, and she looked so very, very sad. Then, without a word, she simply vanished.

"Gwen!" he called to her. "Gwen, come back! I just want to talk to you! To make things right between us!"

But there was no sign of her. Instead, he was standing on a vast and barren plain with no one around for miles. No dinosaurs, no Gwen…no one and nothing. Just him and his regrets.

"Gwen!" he called as his voice seemed to echo and re-echo throughout the nothingness. And when no response came, he started to panic. He was convinced he'd missed his chance to make things right between them.

No! He refused to accept that! He had to find her. He had to make things the way they should be.

And so he started off across the plain, the harsh wind whistling around him. He set out in search of his daughter, intent on making up for his past faults. He and his daughter were going to begin anew, with a clean slate.

Eric suddenly sat up. He was, in fact, in bed in the farmhouse. But he failed to realize this. His eyes were wide open, but he saw none of the reality surrounding him. Instead, he saw only the vast plain and felt the deep-seated need to go out and find Gwen. He had no idea where to look for her, but he didn't waver in his conviction that he could find her.

Cayley was dozing nearby, having fallen asleep on the couch. Gwen's father had no idea that it was she who had been tending him, carefully mopping his brow whenever the fever became too intense. She had stayed up for as long as she could, but the fatigue had finally overcome her.

Eric Corey didn't give his sleeping nurse so much as a glance.

Instead, he rose from his bed. He was bare-chested, wearing only pants. This, however, did not slow him down in the least. He knew the farmhouse well, and he set to doing things as he always did. He pulled on his boots, put on a shirt, and headed out the door into the bright, cheerful sunlight.

Dismo was taking a nap in a nearby field. Eric didn't see the dinosaur. In fact, when he looked in front of him, Eric did not see a field, or a forest in the distance. Instead, he saw only a desert, a desert of fear and sadness that he'd been wandering in for far too long. He was now prepared to do something about it.

And so he set off. At first he walked with something of a stagger, but then he began to recover his stride and moved at a quicker, faster pace. He felt stronger than ever. It was as if he'd never been stronger, more confident than he was at that very moment. It was as if his entire world suddenly made crystal-clear sense.

He was going to find Gwen and make everything right, even if he had to cross the entirety of the desert before him in order to do it.

Cayley woke from her sleep. She stretched like a cat, then opened her eyes, brushing her long hair out of them. She turned toward the bed to see how Gwen's dad was doing.

It took her a few moments to fully register that he wasn't there.

Even then, the significance of that didn't completely hit her. But then she began to fully wake up. "Mr. Corey," she said slowly. Then more loudly, she called, "Mr. Corey!"

Cayley went around to the far side, wondering if maybe he had simply rolled off and was lying on the other side on the floor. But there was no sign of him.

Panic started to well up in her as she remembered what Doctor Traptor had warned.

Keep him away from human contact.

"Oh, my gosh," she said. "Oh, no. I've lost Gwen's dad!"

After a quick inspection of the rest of the farmhouse, Cayley dashed out the front door, shouting Eric's name. There was no sign of him.

"This is terrible!" she cried, looking around frantically. And then she spotted Dismo lying a short distance away, sunning himself. She ran across the field, calling out after him.

He didn't stir. He seemed quite content to lie where he was.

"Dismo!" she screamed as loud as she could. This time, he woke up.

He brought his massive three-horned head up and focused on her. "What is it?" he rumbled.

"It's Gwen's dad! He's gone!"

"Gone? Gone where?"

"I don't know! If I knew where, I'd just go after him!"

Dismo appeared to consider this a moment. "That makes sense," he admitted. "He really shouldn't be wandering around on his own, should he?"

"No, of course not! He shouldn't even be out of bed!"

"Then I guess we have to find him." Dismo hauled himself to his feet in his slow and lumbering fashion. "All right. Climb on."

She hesitated at first, but then clambered up behind Dismo's large bone crest. "Do you know where to look for him?"

"No. But I will," Dismo said. He walked with a measured stride to the farmhouse. Cayley felt as if she were going out of her mind, because Dismo was moving incredibly slowly. However, she knew there was nothing she could say or do to increase the dinosaur's pace.

He sniffed around the door to the farmhouse, then the ground. "What are you doing?" Cayley called down to him.

"Refamiliarizing myself with his scent. Not too difficult, really. I've known him so long that I pretty much know it as well as my own."

"You're going to track him by scent? Like a dog?"

"Dinosaurs don't do things like dogs. Dogs do things like dinosaurs," he reminded her archly. "We were here first, after all!"

With that admonition ringing in her ears, Cayley held on as best she could as Dismo set off in pursuit of the runaway patient.

As they went, Cayley again thought of what Doctor Traptor had said: Eric was very contagious. The disease was capable of spreading. He must remain confined to the farm.

But now Eric Corey was out. What if he infected other people somehow? What if this Zinix disease started to spread? What if large numbers of the human population began to contract the disease?

Not only would there be tremendous loss of life, but it would all be her fault. She was the one who had fallen asleep.

It was, of course, rather harsh for her to blame herself completely. After all, no one could have expected her never to sleep. Still, she could have tied him down or something. But the thought had never occurred to her. He had seemed so harmless lying there, so incapable of even sitting up, much less posing a threat to anyone.

Now, though, it was entirely possible that—if she didn't find him in time—an isolated case could begin a widespread epidemic.

"We've got to find him, Dismo," she said urgently. "We've just got to."

CHAPTER 11

As Booj stood next to his two new companions, Xin's words rang in his head: *"You don't care about anyone other than yourself."*

Booj mused over the fact that words of praise always seemed to slip away as if they had no weight, but criticism stuck with you no matter how much you wanted to shake it loose. *"You don't care about anyone other than yourself."* The words stung.

Booj was smart and knew it beyond any doubt. He liked to have fun, and he liked to show off. But deep down there was a streak of insecurity, and he couldn't help but wonder if perhaps everybody, saurian and human, was like that—that, deep down, everybody had doubts as to whether they were good and true and worthy, and that criticism stuck because one was always concerned that one had somehow been "seen through."

Maybe, he mused, even though we crack the shell and leave the egg, we never truly leave it behind. Inside, we've all got a fearful newborn who finds the world a confusing and scary place.

Booj didn't say any of this out loud, of course. He wasn't about to admit to any insecurities in front of his newfound acquaintances. He was supposed to be their guide. The last thing they needed was to think that their guide was insecure. As Booj saw it, a guide had to be confident, secure in himself, knowledgeable, and never the least bit uncertain.

So as they made their way toward their destination, he was caught slightly off guard when Gwen asked, "What's that whistling?"

He was about to say, "What whistling?" because he couldn't hear anything. But then he listened carefully and realized it was the wind.

"Oh, it's just the wind," Booj said dismissively. "It whistles down these canyon walls all the time. Nothing to worry about."

The walls stretched high and were in a variety of formations. It was all very picturesque. Gwen might have actually found some enjoyment in it if she hadn't been so nervous. She knew that time was passing, and she couldn't help but feel as if every minute spent while her father wasn't cured was a minute wasted. The weather seemed to match her mood as well; after starting out sunny, it had become overcast.

"How do I look?" Booj suddenly asked her. "You haven't said."

He held his arms out to display Jason's black waistcoat. Booj had sliced it partway down the back to give himself more room to maneuver his shoulders. Jason had visibly winced as Booj's claw effortlessly cut through the once-favored waistcoat. But then he mentally shrugged it off, realizing there was nothing he could do about it.

"It's very nice. Very striking. Are we there yet?" Gwen asked with undisguised impatience. "For that matter, where *is* there? We don't really have any idea because you haven't told us."

"I wanted it to be a surprise," insisted Booj. "But don't worry, it's right up ahead."

They turned a corner in the canyon, and Gwen gasped. Jason looked surprised as well.

"Well?" asked Booj. "What do you think? Looks like dinosaur feet to me."

They found themselves standing at the far end of a small field that looked like solid rock but was covered with fossilized dinosaur footprints. Dozens of them, tracked all over and forever locked into place.

"How is this possible?" Jason asked in amazement.

"No one's quite sure," admitted Booj. "One theory is that it was a flow of burned limestone, forming a cementlike layer in which dinosaurs left their marks. Others claim that it was sculpted by an unknown artist as a personal tribute to someone we don't know. One school of thought," and his voice dropped as if he were at a campfire telling frightening stories, "is that ghosts left them. Ghosts of dinosaurs past."

"I think we can safely forget that last one," Jason said confidently. He looked around, walking delicately as he examined the footprints.

Gwen stood there with her arms folded. "All right," she said with resolve. "Now what?" The wind was blowing more fiercely since they had reached their destination, and it kept tossing her hair into her face. She pushed it out of the way for what seemed the umpteenth time and continued, "Where's the Maze, Booj? Are we in the right place?"

"Definitely," said Booj, who wasn't at all sure.

"Think so?" Jason asked skeptically.

"Uh, yes," said Booj.

"Well, I'm not so sure," said Jason.

"Not sure?" Gwen's brow furrowed and she began to pace. Her nerves appeared to be getting the better of her, and the whistling wind didn't seem to be helping. "Well, I think we'd better get sure, and fast! It's not as if time has come to a stop for my father!"

"We're doing the best we can," Jason said reasonably. He crept slowly among the footprints. As he did so, he repeated the poem to remind himself. "You must go in striding to the place of hiding, from the mountain of heated depth, with feet and saurian's breath lit on high, do hide the way inside." He shook his head. "It might still mean the Foothills. We might still be in the wrong place."

"I'm telling you, we're not," Booj said with conviction.

"Okay, fine," Jason said, standing and facing Booj challengingly. "Then you tell me where we should be. Where's the hidden entrance?"

"It's around here somewhere. We just have to have patience."

"Patience is for people with time!" Gwen exclaimed, the fear evident in her voice. Her concern over her father was becoming obvious, and the wind was clearly bothering her. She cast a glance over her shoulder to see where the wind was coming from as she continued, "We're running out of time! Dad is—"

"Gwen, we know you're worried about your dad," Jason said. "But everyone is doing their bes—"

"Look!" Gwen cried. She pointed up toward rock formations at the top of the canyon, approximately fifty feet above them. "Look, look!" she cried again.

Booj and Jason immediately saw what she was pointing at.

"I'll be!" said Jason, impressed and amazed. "Booj, you see what I'm seeing?"

"Definitely," agreed the Raptor.

High above them, whether by careful design or whimsical happenstance of nature, there was a rock formation that looked exactly like the head of a tyrannosaur with its mouth open. Because of its positioning on the canyon wall, it was a channel for the various winds that howled through the passages. The winds were being funneled through a sizable hole that was positioned toward the front of the tyrannosaur's "snout," as bits of debris could be seen flying out.

"Saurian's breath!" Gwen called out joyously. "The wind is coming through there! Right through there! Booj, this *is* the place!" She impulsively hugged the Raptor.

Jason, looking mildly annoyed, stood to one side and muttered, "Well, it was *my* scroll that gave us the clue in the first place."

"Of course it's the place," Booj said confidently, ignoring Jason and enjoying the hug. "I told you it was."

"So…so now what?" asked Gwen. "Where's the entrance? Now that we know for sure, where's the entrance?"

Immediately, they began to inspect the base of the wall where the head was visible. But there didn't seem to be anything that pointed to a hidden entrance.

Jason looked upward and studied the rock formation thoughtfully for a moment. "Maybe—this will sound crazy—but maybe it's in the mouth itself."

"That makes sense. 'Lit on high' might mean that we're supposed to alight up there, and there's some sort of hidden passage," agreed Booj.

As they looked up the rock wall, they realized it wouldn't be the easiest of climbs.

"Booj, can you handle this?" asked Jason. "The climb, I mean?"

"Of course," said Booj, who once again wasn't sure. "What about you?"

"I have my ways. Gwen, you should stay down here, all right?"

"Why? You're not thinking of trying to leave me behind?"

"Of course not," said Jason. "But it's a tricky climb. If it's not going to lead to anything, there's no point in all of us taking the risk. So you should probably just stay here, and we'll see what we find up there. If there *is* a hidden entrance, then you should come up, too."

"Well, all right," Gwen said grudgingly.

Booj started his climb. His natural vaulting ability helped, and although he had a few backslides, his claws dug into the rock with great ease and he hauled himself up.

Jason, in the meantime, had pulled several pieces of something from his all-purpose satchel. Within seconds, he had assembled a hand-held crossbow. The arrow had a rather sharp hook on the end. Attached to the back end of it was a length of cable. He aimed it toward the upper portion of the canyon wall and fired.

The first shot didn't hold, nor did the second. But the third one appeared to lodge solidly into a crevice. Jason pulled on the cable several times, then swung his feet onto the wall so that he could apply his full weight to it. It held with no problem. He then hauled himself up, hand over hand.

As Jason climbed, Booj looked over and said, "You

know, you could have just handed me the hook end and had me climb up. I would have attached it for you."

"I like to do things for myself," Jason said firmly, and Booj nodded. It seemed he and Jason had something in common.

"Whatever you say," Booj replied, deciding perhaps he'd finally found the makings of a true friendship.

From the ground, Gwen watched Jason and Booj with apprehension as they made their way up. Perhaps she should have insisted on going with them, but Jason's reasoning had made sense. Still, it went against the grain for her simply to stand by while others did the work.

Within minutes, the two had reached the top and were climbing around inside the mouth of the tyrannosaur. Gwen called up to them, "Well, do you see anything?"

"Still looking," Jason called back. "The interior's cramped and the walls are solid. We're not seeing anything that looks remotely like a secret entrance."

"Well, you should keep looking then!" Gwen instructed.

Ten minutes later, Booj called down. "Nothing!"

"It's got to be there!" insisted Gwen.

"Well, it's not. If you don't believe us, come look for yourself," called Jason.

"Of course I believe you," Gwen said. Then she sighed and began to pace, heedless of where she was stepping amidst the footprints. In exasperation, she slammed her foot down twice and cried out, "This is so frustrating!"

Suddenly, she heard something that sounded like gears turning. It was coming from a section of rocky wall to her right. She went over to the wall, put her hands against it—

—and the wall whipped around and hurled her into darkness.

Both Booj and Jason had been looking down at Gwen at the moment it happened, and they couldn't believe what they saw.

One moment she was there, the next she was gone. There was now a large hole in the rocky wall where she'd been standing. And Gwen had vanished into it.

CHAPTER 12

There was a thin shaft of light from overhead, but it took Gwen's eyes a few minutes to get adjusted to the darkness. Then she remembered the sunstone goggles. She pulled them from the inside pocket of her cloak and put them on. Immediately, the area snapped into a clearer picture.

What she saw took her breath away.

She was in a vast open area with stairs and walls stretching off in all directions. Some of them seemed almost impossible in the way they fit together. There were ledges overhead and ledges below, extending as far as the eye could see. She was standing on a path that was about nine feet wide. She couldn't tell what it was connected to or where it led in either direction.

And in the distance, she heard the bellowing of what could only be a great beast.

It sounded like the most fearsome of creatures—a low, dull roar that grew in pitch and intensity, and then stopped abruptly. She was somewhat relieved when the roaring ceased and hoped that the thing, whatever it was, would keep its distance from them.

"Gwen!" came Jason's frantic voice. "Gwen, are you down there?"

"Yes, of course!" Gwen called up to him. "Where else would I be?"

"You all right?"

"I've been better!" she announced. "But otherwise I'm fine." As Booj and Jason chattered above her, she stood and dusted herself off, then looked up to see Booj and Jason gazing down at her again. The swiveling door through which she had fallen had opened onto a narrow ledge. Her foot had hit it when she'd come through, but she'd stumbled backward and fallen right off it. Fortunately, the drop was only far enough to bruise her ego rather than cause any real damage.

"We get it now!" Booj called. "The verse!"

"Oh, really," answered Gwen, still dusting herself off.

"Yes, definitely," said Booj.

"Here was the whole trick," explained Jason. "You'll love this. When it talked about 'lit on high,' what it meant was that when the sun was at its highest point in the sky, it would backlight the outcropping that formed the stone dinosaur's mouth, and the shadow would be cast directly on this spot and mark the entrance! Then you just stomp on the ground outside it with your feet, and that sets the opening mechanism into motion. That's what the part about 'striding' relates to. The thing is, since the day was so overcast, there was no shadow from the dinosaur head, so it never occurred to us. So, you see, with all the energy we used to try and figure out the exact wording, here you went and simply stumbled on it. Isn't that funny?"

"Hilarious. I'm splitting my sides. Now will you two get down here already!"

"Oh," said Jason. "Sorry."

Booj turned his back to Gwen and extended his long tail through the opening. Jason slid down it, releasing it when he reached the bottom, and dropping the final couple of feet with no harm. Moments later, Booj leaped down next to them effortlessly.

At that moment, the mysterious creature roared again in the distance. Immediately, Jason's and Booj's heads snapped around. "Wh-what was that?" said Jason, sounding genuinely nervous for the first time since Gwen had met him.

"I don't know," said Gwen. "And I've got a funny feeling that I don't want to know, either."

Jason put on his sunstone goggles as well. As for Booj, his saurian vision came naturally, and his eyes quickly adapted to the darkness on their own. "This place is incredible," gasped Jason. "Look at the size of it! This was obviously constructed for dinosaurs to move through."

"So how do we find Odon?" asked Gwen.

They all looked at each other.

Gwen tilted her head back, cupped her hands on either side of her mouth, and shouted, "Oooodonnn!" Her voice echoed and reverberated throughout the Maze.

No response came.

"It was worth a shot," she said with a shrug.

And then, suddenly, they heard something from overhead. It was the pounding of wings accompanied by a high-pitched screeching.

"What the heck is—?"

From on high, a black mass was moving toward them, at first indistinguishable as anything other than one big...thing. But then it became clearer.

It was a huge flock of Preondactylus. Small, toothy pterosaurs with an eighteen-inch wingspan, looking like a cross between a bat and a barracuda. And the creatures were bearing down on them. Unlike the more highly evolved, intelligent dinosaurs that populated Dinotopia, the Preondactylus were interested in nothing more than satisfying their hunger— and they were descending en masse on the likeliest candidates for that.

"Move! Come on, move!" Jason cried out.

The three of them ran as fast as they could along the ramp.

"Why are they attacking us?!"

"Because, Gwen, your shout probably attracted them! That's why! They were sleeping somewhere, minding their own business, and you woke them up!"

"Well, excuse me, Jason, but it seemed like a good idea at the time, okay?"

"Less talking, more running!" called out Booj.

They rounded a blind corner and found themselves at an intersection. A stairway led up in one direction, and a ramp led off to the left into a sizable hole in the wall. At the right was a dead end.

"Which way?" Gwen asked.

"The stairs!" Booj said with confidence, though Gwen knew he had no more of an idea what was right than she or Jason did.

Clearly Jason didn't care. At the sound of Booj's confident tone, he took the lead and began running up the stairs without a moment's hesitation.

"Wait!" shouted Gwen suddenly. She lunged forward, grabbed Jason by the back of his shirt, and hauled him off the steps. Her timing could not have been better, for at that instant, an array of spikes snapped straight up out of the stairs. Any of them would have punched right through his feet, crippling him.

He looked down at his feet, and then at Gwen. "How did you know?" he asked in amazement.

"Look at the holes in the steps," Gwen replied.

"Oh…thanks," he murmured, aware of just how close his call had been.

"Don't mention it," she replied.

The Preondactylus could be heard squealing not far away.

"How do they survive down here?" Jason wondered. "What do they eat?"

"Little boys named Jason?" suggested Booj.

"Very funny," said Jason.

"Come on!" Gwen urged, hearing the oncoming Preondactylus. "Let's run."

"No," said Booj suddenly. "Crouch low. Stay where you are and crouch low. I know what I'm doing this time, believe me."

"Why?" Gwen asked. "Why should we—"

"There're enough stalactites and cross-ramps around to confuse the Preondactylus in the darkness," Booj explained. "If they don't notice us, then they'll go for the thing that's moving!"

"I get it!" Jason said quickly. "Do as he says, Gwen."

They did as the Raptor suggested, each curling up into as tight a ball as each could manage. Gwen thought her heart would burst out of her chest, it was pounding so hard.

The Preondactylus flapped closer, and then they turned the blind corner and flew right over Jason, Gwen, and Booj. Wheeling around in the air as one, the Preondactylus circled, looking for their prey. But nothing was moving, so they didn't know where to attack.

Suddenly, the sound of the monster in the distance echoed through the cavern, and the Preondactylus squealed and shrieked. In another moment, they were gone, flying off into the darkness of the Maze.

When all was quiet again, Gwen, Jason, and Booj rose to their feet. In silence they moved forward, following a path about thirty feet. Then they turned a corner and stopped dead. There was a large stone door in front of them.

In one section of the door was a series of tumbler locks. The locks had an assortment of crescent and circle shapes over them. Booj tried turning one, but was unable to get a grip on the dial of the lock. His clawed hands could only clack against it. He began to lean forward so that he could grip it with his teeth and attempt to turn it that way.

"I'll do it, Booj," said Jason. His hands hovered over the tumblers. "Think it matters which one I turn first?" He turned the tumbler that was under the fullest circle.

There was a loud *clack* beneath their feet.

"That didn't sound good," observed Gwen.

Suddenly, the far end of the path began to tremble, then break away. In sections, one after the other, it crumbled.

"Doesn't look good, either," she added.

There was no place else for the trio to stand—the stone path was directly under their feet, and there was no door frame for them to hold on to. Unless they could get the door open, the path beneath their feet was going to crumble into nothingness, and they would be sent plummeting into who-knew-what.

"The moon!" Jason suddenly exclaimed.

"Yes, that would definitely be a better place to be," Booj said, watching as their only means of support cracked apart faster and faster.

"No, these symbols! I'm so stupid! They're the phases of the moon! They must have to be turned in the order the moon goes, from waxing to waning!"

Jason's fingers flew over the dials, turning them as rapidly as he could. He tried not to pay attention to the crumbling of the path. The vibrations under his feet were so violent that his hand continually slipped off the dials. But he kept turning.

"Hurry!" shouted Gwen.

"I am!"

"Hurry!"

"I am!"

He twisted the last dial, and with a noise that sounded like smoothly turning gears, the door slid up into the ceiling. Immediately, Gwen, Jason, and Booj leaped into the opening—just as the path behind them fell completely apart.

They stood on the other side of the door and breathed a sigh of relief. "That was close," said Jason.

And then, without warning, the path on the other side of the door crumbled beneath their feet, dumping them into blackness.

CHAPTER 13

The man stumbled out of the woods, looking confused. He was disheveled and drenched in his own sweat.

"Gwen!" he cried. "I'm sorry!"

The girl he was screaming at was not named Gwen. Nor had she ever seen the man who was now lurching toward her. Her name was Harper, and she was crouched by the side of the river washing clothes. She was extremely startled to see the man coming straight at her.

His face was flushed, as if he had run a long way. His eyes burned with an inner fire that appeared to be guiding him through his semiconscious journey. Something about him wasn't quite right, and the freckle-faced girl with straight red hair became very nervous.

Still, she remembered her manners, which were especially important when addressing one's elders. "My name is not Gwen," she said politely. "It's Harper. I'm afraid you've mixed me up with someone else, sir."

He walked up to her, his legs looking as if they were ready to buckle. He sank down onto the grass opposite her, maintaining his balance by keeping his knuckles planted on the ground. "Gwen," he said, as if she hadn't spoken, "can you forgive me?"

"Sir," Harper said, maintaining her patience, "I am not—"

He gripped her by the shoulders. "Can you forgive me!" he demanded, more insistently than before. His hands clasped the cloth of her dress, but not, fortunately, her skin.

It occurred to her that the best way to handle the situation was to tell him what he wanted to hear. So she said, "Um, okay, I forgive you."

Tears began to roll down the man's face. "You—you do?"

"Yes—yes, sure I do."

She reached up to wipe the tears from his eyes. But before she could touch them, the man stood up, turning his face away. "I'm—I'm sorry, honey. I shouldn't let you see me like this."

"It's all right," she told him, still completely confused.

He dried his eyes with his back to her. "I'm your father. I have a responsibility to be strong for you. That's what matters. That's what's important."

Then he lapsed into a long silence. At first, Harper was going to ask him what this was all about, but then she realized it would be better to keep quiet.

"Gwen?" His back was still to her. "Gwen, where are you?"

She realized that this very odd man had totally forgotten that she was standing right behind him. She took this as the perfect opportunity to remain silent.

"Gwen, honey?" he repeated over and over again. As he walked away from Harper, he didn't even look back. It was as if the entire conversation with Harper had slid off into another realm of consciousness. Harper sat down so as not to attract attention to herself. Within minutes, he'd left her behind, staggering away along the riverbank.

"That," she said to no one in particular, "was one of the strangest things that's ever happened to me."

However, Harper wasn't finished with her strange encounters for the day. After drying her laundry on the rocks by the river, she began to feel the ground rumbling at a fairly steady and rhythmic pace, in a manner that immediately indicated to her that a dinosaur was on the way. A four-legged one, judging by the beat of it. She sat up, squinted, and saw a Triceratops in the distance. Judging from the way he dragged his tail, he didn't seem to be a particularly young one, either. And there was a girl riding him, crouched just behind the bony protection around his head. The girl's long hair was bouncing around as the dinosaur trudged along. At one point, the Triceratops paused, seemed to sniff the air, and then kept on moving.

"Hey!" screamed the girl. "We're looking for someone! Can you help us? We're looking for—"

"A man?" questioned Harper as she rose to her feet, dusting herself off. "Has a kind of crazy look to him?"

"Yes!" the girl said excitedly. "Yes, have you seen him?"

"Um, that way," Harper said, and pointed up the river. "Hours ago."

Then the Triceratops took a step closer to her and the girl said, "Did he—did he come into contact with you? Cough on you or anything?"

"What?"

"Did he? It's tremendously important!"

Harper frowned, running the encounter back through her mind. "He grabbed my shoulders at one point. But that was it."

"Insects," the girl said as if struck by a sudden thought. "Have you been bitten by an insect recently?"

"What?"

"Could an insect have bitten him, and then you?"

"I don't think so. I haven't—look, what are you talking about? What's happening?"

The girl and the dinosaur looked at each other. "She should be all right," said the dinosaur, as if Harper hadn't spoken. "If there were going to be any problems, she would be showing them by now, particularly because of her youth. It would happen quickly."

"Do you feel all right?" inquired the girl.

"Yes!" Harper said with growing exasperation. "Yes, I feel fine! Now would one of you like to tell me what's going on?"

The long-haired girl said briskly, "Actually, I'd rather not. But if you start getting any kind of cold symptoms or anything, get hold of Doc TRaptor immediately. Tell him what happened here. He'll understand."

And without a further word, she wheeled the Triceratops around and they headed off down the river.

"Well, I'm glad *someone* will understand," said the utterly perplexed Harper.

"This is bad," Dismo said to Cayley. "I expected bad, but this is really quite bad."

"Why?"

"This is a tributary that leads into the Polongo River," he told her. "And the Polongo feeds into not only Waterfall City, but the Great Canal. If Eric should fall into the river, he could infect all of it."

"How long would the virus be able to survive in the water?"

"Long enough," said Dismo worriedly. "Long enough. Humans bathe in the water, they drink from it. If Eric infects that water, it could wipe out every human being in all of Dinotopia."

CHAPTER 14

Jason tumbled end-over-end, waving his arms, trying to find something he could grab on to. But there was nothing at all to slow his plunge—until something elastic halted his fall. As it stretched beneath him and then slowly snapped back into shape, Jason scrambled around on his hands and knees in an attempt to see where he was. He heard frustrated grunts nearby, and then saw that Gwen and Booj were right there ahead of him.

They appeared to be on a very unsturdy net that trembled beneath them. Jason looked down and shuddered—the net was constructed of intertwining vines and was anchored at four corners. Beneath the net appeared to be a bottomless pit. The only thing preventing them from falling into it—possibly forever—was this very shaky net.

In the distance, the "Monster of the Maze" let out another roar. Jason tried not to think about it.

"Nice and easy," Jason said trying to keep his voice as calm as possible. "What we're going to do is just climb up out of here. That's all…just…climb…up."

"Sounds like an excellent plan," agreed Booj. He saw a narrow ledge above them that angled off into the unseen distance. It was definitely their best bet.

However, as Booj started to climb up toward it, his claws sliced through the vines. The simple act of grasping the vines with his razor-sharp claws caused the vines to break, and it didn't matter how delicately he held them. He was absolutely unable to control it.

"Booj, be careful!" Gwen cried. "If the net gives, we're all dead."

"I *am* being careful!" Booj replied.

"Will the two of you calm down!" Jason yelled. The tension, the constant threat of death, was starting to get to all of them.

Then there was a moment of near disaster as Booj's foot went through one of the newly created holes caused by his taloned toes. The entire safety net lurched.

By this time, Booj was afraid to move. He had made several stabs at doing so, and each one opened up a new means of disaster. "If I try this a few more times," he warned them, "I'll probably cut this net to pieces. So, I have an idea—let's stay here."

"Stay here?" Jason echoed. "That's not a very good plan."

"It's not a brilliant plan," admitted Booj, "but if you have something else in mind, I'm listening."

Jason paused for a moment to survey the situation.

"Wait for us to get to where you are," he told Booj. "Come on, Gwen, we have to help him."

Gwen nodded and the two of them crawled very carefully on their hands and feet until they reached the spot where Booj was.

"We're here, Booj," Jason said. "Now hop on!"

"What?" Booj exclaimed.

"*What?*" Gwen echoed.

"Put one foot on each of our backs," Jason continued. "It's the most reasonable way to go. Just balance yourself carefully and try not to dig your claws into us."

"What do you mean, *try* not to?" Gwen blurted.

"Are you sure about this?" Booj asked.

"Not really, Booj. But I trust you," Jason told him encouragingly. "Gwen, don't you trust him?"

Gwen swallowed. "Sure. Sure I do."

"No, she doesn't," said Booj. "She's just saying that."

"I'm not," said Gwen after a moment. "You saved our lives on the river, Booj. Now it's our turn to help you."

"Really?" asked Booj, as if no one had ever offered to do him a good turn.

"Really," said Jason, then he smiled. "We're a team now, aren't we?"

"A team," whispered Booj. "I like the sound of that."

"Then let's go," urged Jason.

Booj nodded and delicately stepped onto Jason's back with his right foot and then eased his left foot onto Gwen's back. The vines creaked heavily beneath them, but none broke, at least for that moment. Booj was poised on the balls of his feet, swaying slightly but maintaining his balance. "It's done," he said nervously, "I'm on."

"Here we go," called Jason. "Gwen, come on, one hand at a time. One...two...three...four..."

Gwen and Jason moved in synch, each hand movement matching the numbers he called out. Booj wavered, but was able to use his tail as a balance whenever he thought he was about to topple over.

Gwen held her breath as safety drew near. The entire time she was concerned that—at the last moment—the vines would suddenly snap, causing them all to fall into the pit. She was also worried that her back was going to break. And having Booj's razor-sharp claws so near her face didn't do much to improve her nerves, either.

"Almost there," Booj said encouragingly as he rode them like twin surfboards. "Allllmost there..."

As soon as they drew close to the edge, Booj vaulted from them. Gwen gasped as the weight was suddenly lifted from her shoulders. Booj landed with a comforting thud, and then extended his tail so that she and Jason could haul themselves up the rest of the way, which is exactly what they did.

"I wonder where we are now," Gwen said as she

patted the dirt off her clothes. "What do you think?"

"Well, we're still in the Maze. That much hasn't changed," said Jason.

There was a stairway leading to the left and a path to the right. From the left, once again, the monster roared.

"You know, there's something about that monster," Gwen said thoughtfully. "Something I can't quite put my finger on."

"Well, while you're trying to decide where to put your finger, let's head this way," Jason suggested, pointing to the right. It certainly seemed like a reasonable suggestion, considering it was in the opposite direction from where the monster apparently was residing.

They moved quickly through the Maze, Booj taking the lead. After a short time, Booj stopped. "Hold it. Do you hear that?"

The two humans strained their ears but couldn't detect anything at first. "What are we supposed to be hearing?" asked Gwen. She felt slightly woozy for some reason, but wasn't sure why.

"A faint hissing of some sort," Booj said uncertainly. "Don't know what's causing it, but it seems to be coming from nearby."

"I don't understand why you're saying that." Something about Jason's voice had changed. He sounded suspicious all of a sudden. "Why would you be saying that? Are you trying to scare me? What did Gwen tell you?"

"Me?" said Gwen in confusion, her annoyance quickly growing for some unknown reason. "What do I have to do with anything?"

"You told Booj you thought I was a coward, didn't you."

"I said no such thing!"

"You certainly have a lot of insecurity for someone who acts like he knows a lot," Booj said.

"Hey, we just bailed you out of a difficult situation," Jason warned him. "Don't you understand that? Why are you challenging my authority?"

"Your authority?" Gwen now spoke up, sounding astonished. "I practically had to drag you along on this expedition, and now *you're* talking about authority?"

They stopped in the middle of the Maze and continued to argue, their voices rising in anger and intensity. It was as if every concern, no matter how minor, had been elevated to gigantic proportions.

Their arguments continued into name-calling and accusations until Jason finally shouted, "Okay, fine! I don't have to work with either of you! I'm going back this way!"

"Oh, no you don't!" countered Gwen. "I'm going back this way! You go ahead the other way!"

"And which way does that leave me?" demanded Booj.

There were high walls on either side, and Jason pointed upward and said, "Go up there! You think you're above us anyway. So go!"

"Fine!" And Booj leaped upward, vaulting the distance easily, and landed on the top of the wall. He turned to gaze back down at the humans.

"Why did you do that?" Gwen asked Jason, her eyes narrowing. "You were just trying to get rid of him, weren't you? Think maybe you're going to pull a fast one, is that it? Well, you're not going to get away with it, I can tell you that right now!"

"I am so sick of listening to you!"

"Not as sick as I am of listening to *you!*"

They were shouting so loudly and intensely that the veins were standing out on their necks. Finally, Jason threw up his hands and said, "Good-bye, then!"

"Good-bye!"

"And I couldn't care less if I never saw you again!"

"I feel exactly the same!"

"In fact, I actually *hope* that I never see you again!"

"So do I!"

"Hold it, the both of you!"

The two looked up at Booj, who was crouched on the overhead wall, feeling very confused. "Why are we arguing like this? I don't get it…"

"She started it!"

"The heck I did. You did!"

"Did not!"

"Did—"

"That hissing!" Booj said suddenly. "I know what it is now! It's probably some sort of natural gas, pouring into this section of the Maze. And it's playing on our fears and uncertainties. It's making us suspicious of one another! The whole idea is that it breaks up teams trying to pass through the Maze, making it impossible for anyone to work together. It's not affecting me now because I'm up above it!"

"Why should I believe you?" asked Gwen.

"You mean, why should we believe him?" Jason corrected her.

"Think about it!" urged Booj. "We may have had some minor differences until now, but there hasn't been open warfare! Does splitting up really make any sense? Well, does it? The only way we'll make it through this place is if we work together, and the *last* thing we should do is go our separate ways!"

Gwen and Jason struggled to cut through the haze that had settled over their brains. "He makes sense," Jason said reluctantly.

"It figures you would say that," Gwen told him. But she sounded less than certain.

"Tell you what," said Booj craftily. "You'd love to prove me wrong, wouldn't you? Shove my snout in it?"

On this the two agreed immediately.

"All right, then," Booj said. "Just keep walking, but stay together. If I'm right, then sooner or later, we'll make it out of this area and return to normal. If I'm wrong—"

"How do we know what normal is?" asked Gwen.

Rather than embark on a lengthy debate, Booj tried some simple reverse psychology. "You're right," he said. "You couldn't possibly know what normal is."

"Oh, yes we could!" shot back Jason immediately. "Come on, Gwen, let's go!"

"I'll go first!" she told him.

He looked about to argue it, but then seemed to give up. "Fine, fine, you go first," he told her with exasperation. She promptly headed out ahead of him. They continued to bicker the entire time.

Booj moved along the top of the wall like a tightrope walker. As he progressed, the wall became very narrow. Eventually, it was impossible for him to maintain his balance. He dropped down into the Maze next to Gwen and Jason and hoped that he wouldn't regress into arguments along with them.

He needn't have worried. He could almost see the suspicious, confused, and twisted expressions leaving Gwen and Jason, as if shrouds were being pulled off. Their belligerent tones began to fade, and it was soon clear that they were wondering why they had been snapping at each other in the first place.

"I feel funny," Gwen said finally. "Like—like there was a buzzing in my head that's gone away now."

"Me too," Jason said.

"Wow. We agree on something."

"I'm not sure what got into me," Jason told her. He looked uncertainly at Booj. "Some sort of gas, you said?"

"That's my theory, yes."

"Nasty stuff."

"Very much so."

"Gwen," Jason said slowly, "I—I said some things, and I want to—"

"No apology necessary," Gwen replied. "I was being less than generous myself. Foul place, this Maze. Finds all sorts of different ways to trip you up."

"Yes," Booj spoke up, "but we'll find ways around whatever it tosses at us. As long as we're a *team*. Agreed?"

The two humans looked at each other, then at Booj. And all three friends nodded in affirmation. Then they continued on with their jorney.

The pathway they chose seemed to be narrowing in front of them, and about ten feet ahead was a bridge. Gwen didn't think it looked particularly inviting, but there didn't seem to be another option. "What do you think?" she asked.

"There's heat rolling up from ahead," Booj said. "I can feel it even through my scales."

"I feel it, too," said Jason. "Heat coming up from below as well. Maybe it's some sort of lava field or something."

"Great, just what we needed," muttered Booj. "A narrow bridge over a lava field. Two of my favorite things combined."

Booj went first, with Jason right behind him. Gwen brought up the rear.

"Watch your step. I don't like the looks of this. This setup smells like week-old meat," Booj murmured.

"I couldn't agree more," said Jason.

Gwen was about to chime in when suddenly she felt something shift beneath her foot. She lifted it slowly to discover that she had just stepped on some sort of pedal, and it had clicked beneath her.

"Guys, there's something here on the ground. I think I just set something off."

"Maybe it won't be so bad," Jason said with less than full conviction in his voice.

His lack of enthusiasm was quickly justified as something slid into place overhead. Moments later, lethal projectiles were hurtling down at them.

The quartz crystals were large, sharp, and falling like hailstones—and that was the good news.

CHAPTER 15

Eric Corey had slumped down near the riverbank.

Cayley saw him from a short distance. He was staring at the cool, rushing river. She knew that a man with a hot fever would probably like nothing better than to slip in for a refreshing dip. But if he did, all of Dinotopia's water supply could be contaminated with the man's illness.

The sick man hauled himself to his feet and began to stagger toward the bubbling river. He moved a couple of feet and then fell to the ground two yards shy. An insect was buzzing around his face, and he tried to wave it away.

He started to stand once more, but couldn't find the strength. Instead, he began pulling himself toward what he clearly saw as a source of relief.

"No!" screamed Cayley as she leaped off Dismo's back. She approached Eric as slowly and carefully as possible.

"Mr. Corey," she said cautiously.

He was staring blankly at her.

"Mr. Corey—remember me? Cayley? Gwen's friend?"

"Gwen?"

"Mr. Corey, you need to back away from the river now. Okay? Just back away from it..."

It was as if her words reminded him of his goal, which was certainly not what she had intended. "River...water...so cool..."

His voice was so raspy that it was barely audible. But judging from the direction he was crawling, Cayley definitely understood his intent. "You're thirsty. That's okay. Tell you what—I'll take you back to your house, and you can have all the water you want there, okay?"

She never stopped moving. As she drew closer and closer, she spoke to him with a constant stream of encouragement. "Everything's going to be fine. Just come with me. Dismo is here, he'll give you a lift. It'll all work out, you'll see." And slowly, she became convinced that he was too far gone to pose any sort of genuine threat.

It was a bad miscalculation on her part.

From out of nowhere, Eric seemed to draw on unexpected reserves of strength, and suddenly he was on his feet. Before Cayley could react, he was staggering toward the river, making inarticulate sounds.

By that point, he didn't even noticed that an insect had landed on his forearm.

Cayley covered the distance between the two of

them with several quick steps. Eric was within a foot of the water when Cayley slammed into him like a football player, knocking him down to the ground.

Eric struggled in her grasp. Under ordinary circumstances, she wouldn't have had a prayer against the much bigger and older man, but between his weakened condition and her sense that she was fighting for the life of every human being in Dinotopia, she managed to keep him away from the river.

Finally, Dismo made it to her side. "What would you like me to do?" he inquired.

"Sit on him!" grunted Cayley from between clenched teeth.

"I don't think that would be advisable," he pointed out.

Cayley didn't bother to mention that she was kidding, because Eric's struggles were slowly ceasing. Within moments, the final exertions had drained him completely, and he slumped over and lay still.

"Okay—help me stand him up," Cayley said with a grunt.

Dismo angled his head down, sliding one of his horns under Eric's back. Cayley managed to reposition Eric so that he was draped across both horns. Then Dismo tilted his head back and Eric slid against Dismo's bone crest—draped across the Triceratops's face.

"Are you all right?" Dismo asked.

"I'm fine," she said. "In fact, I was pretty luck— ow!"

Her hand slapped down reflexively on her arm, and she saw the crushed remains of an insect, with a swelling already growing where it had bitten her. A small circle of blood was welling up on her skin.

She looked at the sweating Eric—and saw a similar swelling at the base of his throat.

"Did this bug bite him?" she asked Dismo.

"I don't know. It's possible."

"If it did, then how bad is the trouble I'm in?"

"Pretty bad," Dismo said evenly. "We'd better get back to the farmhouse while you can still walk."

"Am I—" She could barely find the words. "Am I going to die?"

"Yes," Dismo told her. "All things die. Sooner or later, you will, too. The question is whether or not you're going to die within days. And the answer to that, I'm afraid, lies entirely with Gwen and Jason."

Cayley looked down in disbelief. She wasn't ready for this at all.

Then Dismo added, "You did well here, Cayley. You should be proud."

CHAPTER 16

Gwen felt someone leaning over her. Slowly, her eyes fluttered open and she looked up to see Jason's face near hers. He drew his head back, and she blurted, "What are you doing!"

He seemed to sag back in relief. "You're all right."

"Yes," she said slowly. "What were you doing? Trying to kiss me?"

"No! I was trying to see if you were still breathing."

"Oh." Gwen sat up and rubbed her eyes. "What exactly happened?"

"After the crystals fell, one end of the bridge snapped. Booj had to haul us up. You were so overwhelmed you passed out."

"Oh," she said again.

"Gwen, are you sure you're all right?" Jason asked. "All you keep saying is *Oh*."

"Oh?"

Jason looked alarmed a moment, then Booj

squawked. "She's teasing you, Jason. Look at her eyes."

"Gwen?" Jason intoned sternly.

"I'm fine, Jason," she said with a little smile, then she winked at Booj. "Thanks for hauling me up."

Booj shuffled a bit bashfully. "You're welcome."

Suddenly, the group started. The monster was again roaring. "Does he always have to do that?" Jason asked. "Doesn't he ever sleep, or get tired of bellowing like that? It's so irritating!"

"Wait a minute," Gwen said, then she began counting aloud.

"What are you doing?" Jason asked her.

"Shh!" she said and kept counting. Booj and Jason looked at each other in confusion.

When she reached 127, the monster roared in the distance. She promptly started from zero and began counting all over again.

Jason seemed to give up trying to figure out what she was doing and instead simply sat down and folded his arms, clearly hoping that this odd compulsion of hers would end at some point in the near future.

She reached 130...and the monster sounded off again.

Slowly, Jason and Booj looked at each other in understanding. Gwen was counting again, and this time Jason joined in. It wasn't really necessary—obviously she knew how to count. It was more like a vote of solidarity. A chance for more teamwork.

They hit 127, and the monster roared once more.

"Okay, that can't be coincidence," Jason said.

"What are the odds," Gwen wondered out loud, "of a creature roaring at regular intervals like that?"

"Almost nonexistent. But what could it be then?"

Gwen's mind raced, trying to come up with an answer. Then her eyes widened and she blurted out, "Water!"

"What?" said a confused Booj.

"I've been doing reading on water sources, like underground water and groundwater, because I was researching irrigation to try and talk my dad into—" Realizing she was getting off the subject at hand, she exclaimed, "I think what we're hearing is a geyser!"

"Of course!" Jason said. "A fissure, a deep crack in the ground, filled with groundwater that's superheated and forced up a narrow channel, blowing upward with hot water and steam. It blows until it runs out of steam, then sort of recharges and blows again. That's what we've been hearing! Except from this distance, it sounds like a monster."

"So naturally we keep heading *away* from it," Booj realized, looking as disappointed as Jason that it hadn't occurred to him first. "If I was constructing this maze and wanted to keep everyone away from the center, I'd make sure to have the center be the last place that anyone would want to get to—"

"Because they think there's something there that's

terrifying," continued Jason. "So they stay away from it. Of course, *of course!*"

"You're saying that you think Odon is where the geyser is," Gwen said to Jason.

"Why not? A ready-made source of water for washing and drinking. The sound of the geyser going off to keep intruders away. Yes, I think if he's anywhere, he's there. Let's go."

From that moment on, they felt as if nothing could get in their way, even the most difficult of problems the Maze had to offer.

"You know," Jason said reflectively, "the biggest challenge of this place is not the physical obstacles, but rather the obstacle that our own imaginations conjure up. We believed that there was some monster blocking the way, and so we kept heading away from where we really wanted to go. But now that we're heading in the right direction, we can't be stopped."

Every so often, if they thought they were losing their bearings, they would pause and wait for the geyser to sound off again. Those were the toughest times for Gwen, because she wanted to remain in motion and find this Odon and learn what he knew. Now that their quest seemed on the verge of being resolved, the reality of just how much was riding on Odon's existence truly began to dawn on her. He was not only her main chance, he was her only chance. If he wasn't there, then her father was as good as dead.

The geyser blasted off again. This time it was so close that the three of them jumped. They began to race through the final twists and turns of the Maze, almost recklessly. If there had been any deathtraps in their path, they would have been in serious trouble. As it was, though, they rounded a final corner—

—and then stopped dead in their tracks.

They were standing in the middle of the Maze. The cavern roof stretched so high that it looked like the night sky. The area was huge. It must have been made to accommodate thousands of dinosaurs.

Still, it wasn't a smooth and open area. There were assorted outcroppings of rock that prevented a clear view of the interior. "I don't like this," Booj said slowly. "We can't see very far."

"Don't worry," said Jason. "We're just looking for one old healer. He can't be too much trouble once we find him."

"Yes, so let's find him," Gwen said simply, then she cupped her hands to her mouth and shouted, "Oooodoooon!"

Her voice reverberated through the center area, but there was no response. So the three entered slowly, looking around, and Gwen shouted the name again. Still, there was no reply.

Gwen began to feel the first stirrings of panic that Odon might be long gone. But rather than think of that possibility and what it would mean, she turned her mind to something fairly harmless. "Where do you think the geyser is?"

And suddenly, they got their answer.

About fifty feet to their right, the ground suddenly rumbled and then disgorged a staggeringly intense burst of water and steam. It shot toward the very top of the cavern. The roar was deafening. The trio moved away from it, putting their hands over their ears, and suddenly they became aware of intense heat behind them.

The area they were standing on came to an abrupt drop-off about twenty feet away. Slowly, they made their way to the edge and looked down. Below them—closer than they would have liked—they could see that the ground was broken up, giving them a view of what was below it.

Lava.

Except this time, it wasn't hardened. This lava was flowing, and it looked extremely vicious.

Jason let out a low whistle. "It's a lava tube," he said, "a channel that brings molten lava directly to a volcano or something. That's probably what helps to superheat the geyser."

"Great," said Gwen. "This is all interesting, Jason. But it still doesn't tell us where we can find—"

"*Look out!*"

The warning was shouted by Booj, and it caught

them completely off guard. They whirled, and couldn't believe what they saw charging straight toward them.

It was a Megaraptor. Twenty-three feet long—thirteen feet longer than Booj! He leaped forward, his teeth bared, his claws extended.

And he was heading straight toward Booj.

CHAPTER 17

"Run!" Booj shouted to Gwen and Jason as he braced himself to meet the charge of the large Megaraptor.

And then, to their astonishment, the Megaraptor suddenly skidded to a halt. There was still an air of menace about him, but he tilted his head slightly to one side and then the other, as if he was studying some sort of microorganism.

"Why are you telling them to run?" asked the Megaraptor.

"I…" Booj was puzzled at the question. He glanced at Gwen and Jason, but they shrugged in equal confusion. "I…thought you were attacking."

"Oh, pardon." The Megaraptor's voice was thin and reedy, indicating extreme age. "It's just been quite some time since I've seen another dinosaur. I suppose my greeting seemed rather…aggressive. My fault. Sorry."

He bobbed his head. "Well…pleasure to meet you all. You can leave now."

With that, he turned his head and started to walk away.

"Wait!" called Gwen. "Are you…Odon?"

The Megaraptor stopped in his tracks and turned to look back at her. "Why…yes…"

She gasped, feeling a rushing of blood in her temples, as if she were giddy or at a very high altitude. "We've…we've been looking for you!"

"Well, you have been looking in vain. I have no time for visitors."

"We need to speak with you, to learn from you," Jason said.

"You are not worthy to be my student. Please go away and leave me in silence."

"Wait," called Booj.

Odon turned to look at the young Raptor. "Why?"

"Well…" Booj shifted uncomfortably from one foot to the other. "They need your help."

"The humans?" Odon asked. He turned to survey them, then turned back to Booj. "I suppose it is only natural. We are the stronger and they are the weaker, so they naturally always look to us for help. That's what happens when nature improperly throws two species together."

"But it's not improper," Gwen spoke up. "Humans and dinosaurs have accomplished great things together. Incredible things. Things that none of us could have accomplished alone."

"True," said Booj. "After all, we three made it here. And, I must admit, as much as I like to boast about accomplishing things on my own, I couldn't have done it without them."

Odon sighed heavily. "We saurians were doing just fine before the humans arrived, and, philosophically speaking—"

"That's not important now," Gwen said, thinking only of her father needing help.

"Important?" challenged Odon, clearly annoyed with Gwen's blurted interruption. "Perhaps not to you, but it is to me. Now, if you'll excuse me, I shall bid you good day."

He started to walk away, but Jason charged forward. "You don't understand, sir, let me explain—"

"Please, get out of my way," Odon said levelly.

It seemed to Gwen, standing a few feet away, that the Megaraptor's patience was beginning to fray.

"No," said Jason firmly. "I apologize for disturbing you, Odon, but you're a healer and you're needed. Gwen's father is ill. We won't leave until you agree to come back with us. To do what's right."

"Don't lecture me on what is right, hatchling," Odon said sharply. "I walked the earth before your great-great-great-great-grand anything was even born. I know more than you could hope to, have given up more than you can believe, have lost more than—"

He stopped and shook his head. "I've been polite, and I've been patient, but now I want to be left alone.

There are always other healers. Seek *them*."

Then, with an impatient turn of his body, the large Megaraptor swept Jason aside with his tail, sending him tumbling away as if he weighed no more than a flea.

He started to move forward, but Booj sprang forward to block his path. "You must listen," Booj insisted. "*You* are the only healer that can help. As I said, we worked as a team to get here, and—"

"So?"

"So!" Gwen took up the argument, stepping behind Odon. "That should prove that humans and saurians can work together!"

"I don't argue that they can't. For instance, I can rip your saurian friend here to pieces," Odon pointed out with a forced calm that chilled Gwen as he said it. "But that doesn't mean I should."

"I...would have to agree with you about that one," Booj said nervously.

"You are wasting your time," Odon continued, "and if there is one thing that I hate above everything else, it's waste."

"What about wasted opportunity, then?" Gwen countered.

"I've had enough of this. Get out of my way," Odon demanded to Booj.

But the young Raptor didn't budge. Instead, he steadied himself against the much larger dinosaur. "No. They need your help."

"Fine," growled Odon, and he headed in another direction, but then Jason blocked his way once more. He turned in another, and there was Gwen.

"We risked our lives to find you," Gwen said urgently. "And we're determined. We're not going to walk away now just because you've got some stupid idea that humans and dinosaurs shouldn't be friends! Maybe you know a lot about healing. Maybe more than anybody. But there're lots of things you obviously don't know, and we're going to tell you about them and keep telling them until you see it our way! So you might as well—"

"*I might as well what?*" And when he spoke, it was with a full-throated roar, so loud that it was almost impossible to understand what he was saying. "I've had enough of this, do you hear? *Enough!*"

Then, like a cornered animal, Odon swung around and charged straight at Booj. The Megaraptor plowed into Booj, knocking him to the ground, and pinning him down with his heavy foot. Gwen's shriek was swallowed up by the larger Raptor's deafening roar.

"That isn't civilized behavior!" Booj shouted, but Odon didn't seem interested in listening. He held Booj to the ground with his deadly 12 inch long claw poised above his ribs.

"Leave him alone!" shouted Gwen as she launched herself at Odon. "Stop it, stop it, let him go! He's our friend!" she cried, beating her fists uselessly against the heavy saurian. Her efforts were valiant, but her blows were no more than little taps against the large Megaraptor.

Jason had already launched himself at Odon's tail. "Let him go!" cried Jason, his voice blending with Gwen's.

"Get out of here!" Booj shouted to his new friends. "Run! Jason, Gwen, run! You can't help me! Save yourselves!"

But neither of them did.

And then, all of a sudden, Odon stilled. Next he lifted his foot away from Booj, who scrambled safely away.

Seeing their friend back on his feet again, Gwen and Jason stopped fighting and simply stood there, watching and waiting.

Odon backed away. Tilting his head, he regarded Gwen and Jason with open curiosity.

"You wanted us to run away, didn't you?" asked Gwen softly. "You wanted to see if we'd abandon our friend, if we'd run and leave him to his fate."

"But he's our friend," said Jason. "And we'd never leave him."

Booj blinked. "Thank you," he whispered. "I feel the same about you."

The Megaraptor remained still. He wasn't charging Booj. He wasn't roaring. He wasn't doing anything.

What he appeared to be doing was thinking.

"Let me tell you a story," Jason suddenly said. "A story we heard, a very sad story. There once was a dinosaur who was a great healer. He drew his strength from nature, which was also the source of his cures. He believed in the natural order of things, and he lived on an island of beauty with others of his kind. On this island were others not of his kind. They were called humans. The healer did not believe that the two were meant to be together. He believed it was unnatural and would lead to bad things. But the other dinosaurs disagreed with him. They saw no harm in this alliance. And because the healer wanted to believe the best of all living things, he supported the alliance, even though he felt it to be wrong. But then a terrible thing happened..."

Jason paused. "What was it, Odon?"

"A pox," said Odon softly after a long silence. "It was a terrible disease brought to the island by a human. A disease that was carried to my species of dinosaur. There was no way to stop it. None of my cures did anything against it. I could only stand by helplessly and watch my friends and relatives succumb to the illness. The only way to stop it was by quarantine. It was one of the greatest tragedies in the history of the island. The infected dinosaurs and humans were moved to an isolated area, and there they remained... until they...until they died...." said Odon, with infinite sadness in his voice.

"When the last of the ill drew the last of their breaths, then the area was burned. Burned so that their infected bodies could not pass the disease on to anyone else. The air was thick with black smoke for days. The land became blackened as well. Dinosaurs came from miles around to pay their respects, to see the black smoke high in the air and mourn for their fallen fellows. Each day they would come and go, come and go—"

"And you watched it all, didn't you?" Jason asked.

The Megaraptor was slowly nodding. Gwen was watching his face carefully. Saurians did not, as a rule, have expressive faces, but she was certain that she could see conflict in his eyes. These were matters that he clearly didn't want to dwell on, for they were so long ago—and yet they had held control of him for all these years.

"When the smoke finally faded," said Odon, "I left. I feared that humans would be the downfall of dinosaurs. That no good could ever come from any association between the two. And I hid myself away in the heart of this great Maze, so I would not have to see the end."

"But there was no end," Gwen said gently. "There was only good. Wisdom, happiness, friendship and… and…"

"Teamwork," Booj finished for her. "Cooperation."

Gwen smiled at him. "Look at us now," she said, "and tell us what you see."

Odon fixed her with a hard gaze, and for a moment, Gwen was positive that all was lost. And then in a voice that sounded surprisingly gentle, the healer said, "I saw two humans, without hesitation, try to save a dinosaur when they could have run away and saved themselves. It's rather amazing, really. And it seemed almost…natural."

"Of course it's natural," Gwen told him.

There was another long silence. Odon stared deep into Gwen's eyes. Gwen remained poised, looking straight back at the Megaraptor. And then Odon said, "So, tell me, what's wrong with your father?"

CHAPTER 18

Dr. Traptor studied the dark green liquid that sat in a vial on the table in the Corey farmhouse. "Amazing," he said. "What did you say it's made from again?"

"A fungus that grows near volcanic vents in my former home," Odon said. "I call it Firelite. Firelite, combined with several other herbs that young Jason here showed me."

Jason, who had been mixing the medication under Odon's watchful eye, smiled. He was busy tending Eric, who lay on his bed with the worst of the disease already gone. His color had returned, the fever had broken.

Gwen and Cayley sat nearby. Cayley was resting her head on Gwen's shoulder, relieved that the ordeal was finished. And, for Cayley, it couldn't have happened at a more opportune time—she had felt the first onslaught of the disease just as the odd grouping of Gwen, Jason, a Velociraptor wearing a black waistcoat, and an enormous Megaraptor carrying a medicine bag over his shoulder showed up at the door.

At that moment, the Megaraptor healer named Odon was engaged in an intense discussion with the other Megaraptor, Ulla, who served as Trapp's assistant and mount. The truth was that Ulla was not the most ambitious Megaraptor in the world—built for speed, something of a premier athlete, and very kind, but she'd never applied herself to becoming more than Dr. Trapp's assistant. Ulla appeared extremely impressed by the calm, confident intelligence of Odon. It seemed as if he was giving her something to aspire to.

No less impressed was the human Dr. Trapp, who had returned to check on Eric's progress, or lack thereof. "I cannot tell you," he said to Odon, "how relieved I am. There is nothing more frustrating than knowing that a patient is suffering and that you can do little to help."

"Yes, I can understand how that feels," Odon said. "I can understand more than you can possibly believe."

"If you don't have any other plans," Dr. Trapp said, "I thought you might want to return with me to my main office. I'd be most intrigued to—"

"Actually," Odon cut him off politely, "I've already made other plans."

"Oh?" said the doctor, with his eyebrow raised.

"Odon is going to be staying with me for a while," Jason said, with undisguised enthusiasm.

"I am rather impressed with young Jason," Odon said. "His knowledge of herbs and the expertise with which he prepared the serum are quite impressive. And, since he has a wealth of reading material, it might be a nice way to catch up with what has been going on in my…absence."

"Ah," said Dr. Trapp.

"Yes," said Odon, "I've had very little contact with society for some time now. I venture out to the surface very rarely. However, I think it's time I re-evaluate my life. Embark again on the maze that relationships with others always are. However, rather than throw myself right into the thick of it, I shall spend time with Jason. It will be a good way to ease myself back into your world."

"You have a standing invitation, then," the doctor told him. He turned to Gwen and said, "I'll be checking back on your father in a day or so. Let him rest, let his body recover. You take it easy too, Cayley. It was a close call for you, as well."

"Believe me, I know," she said.

Dr. Trapp and Ulla left after a few minutes, and then Jason took Gwen's hand. "I'll be back, too," he said.

"That…would be nice," she replied.

Gwen then turned to Odon and hugged him.

"I don't know how I can ever repay you," she said.

"I feel the same toward you," Odon replied graciously.

The moment the door closed behind them, Cayley

turned to Gwen and grinned, "I think Jason likes you. I can tell."

"Oh, don't be ridiculous. We're just friends," retorted Gwen, but inwardly, she smiled.

"Gwen?"

She turned upon hearing her father's voice. He still looked weak, but clearly he was recovering. She went to his side and knelt down next to him. "You're going to be okay, Dad. They found a cure for you."

"You mean *you* found a cure. I heard them. You risked everything for me."

"And I'd do it again."

He managed a smile. "Things are going to be different around here, Gwen. I should've treated you better. But there's one thing you've got to believe. For all the mistakes I've made, none of them were made because I didn't love you. I always have, and always will."

"I know, Dad."

He hugged her tightly and then said, "This irrigation thing you were trying to tell me about—I want to hear more about it. It'll take some work to get it done, though. Hope Dismo's up for it."

"That shouldn't be a problem," Gwen said. "While you've been sick, I found Dismo an assistant. I think they're going to get on very well together."

"You did? That's great, honey! Who did you—?"

A loud thud came from the door. Gwen immediately recognized it as Dismo rapping with his horns. She walked over, opened the door, and gasped at the sight that awaited her.

Dismo was standing there with brightly decorated ribbons tied all over his horns.

"I was taking a nap," he rumbled, "and when I woke up, these *things* were all over me."

Booj stepped in behind Dismo. "Gwen said you needed some cheering up. As your new assistant, I've decided to make it my first assignment."

Dismo grumbled.

"What's the matter?" asked Booj innocently. "I always find a bit of bright color cheers *me* up."

Gwen surveyed the elderly Triceratops. "Actually, Dis, I think it becomes you."

Dismo shook his head, though Gwen was sure she saw a sparkle of amusement in his eye.

Cayley and Eric remained speechless, but Gwen assured them it would all work out just fine. "Of course," she told them with a shrug, "there'll probably be a brief period of adjustment."

Look for these other Dinotopia titles...

WINDCHASER
by Scott Ciencin

During a mutiny on a prison ship, two very different boys are tossed overboard—and stranded together on the island of Dinotopia. Raymond is the kindhearted son of the ship's surgeon. He immediately takes to this strange new world of dinosaurs and befriends a wounded Skybax named Windchaser. Hugh, on the other hand, is a sly London pickpocket who swears he'll never fit into this paradise.

While Raymond helps Windchaser improve his shaky flying, Hugh forms a sinister plan. Soon all three are forced into a dangerous adventure that will test both their courage and their friendship.

RIVER QUEST
by John Vornholt

Magnolia and Paddlefoot are the youngest pairing of human and dinosaur ever to be made Habitat Partners. Their first mission is to discover what has made the Polongo River dry up, and then—an even more difficult task—they must restore it to its usual greatness. Otherwise, Waterfall City, which is powered by energy from the river, is doomed.

Along the way Magnolia and Paddlefoot meet Birch, a farmer's son, and his Triceratops buddy, Rogo, who insist on joining the quest. Together, the unlikely four must battle the elements, and sometimes each other, as they undertake a quest that seems nearly impossible.

HATCHLING
by Midori Snyder

Janet is thrilled when she is made an apprentice at the Hatchery, the place where dinosaur eggs are cared for. But the first time she has to watch over the eggs at night, she falls asleep. When she wakes up, one of the precious dinosaur eggs has a crack in it—a crack that could prove fatal to the baby dinosaur within.

Afraid of what people will think, Janet runs away, hoping to find a place where no one knows of her mistake. Instead, she finds Kranog, a wounded hadrosaur. Kranog is trying to return to the abandoned city of her birth to lay her egg, but she can't do it without Janet's help. Now Janet will have to face her fears about both the journey ahead and herself.

LOST CITY
by Scott Ciencin

In search of adventure, thirteen-year-old Andrew convinces his friends, Lian and Ned, to explore the forbidden Lost City of Dinotopia. But the last thing they expect to discover is a group of meat-eating Troodons!

For centuries, this lost tribe of dinosaurs has lived secretly in the crumbling city. Now Andrew and his friends are trapped. They must talk the tribe into joining the rest of Dinotopia. Otherwise, the Troodons may try to protect their secrets by making Andrew, Ned, and Lian citizens of the Lost City...for good!

SABERTOOTH MOUNTAIN
by John Vornholt

For years, sabertooth tigers have lived in the Forbidden Mountains, apart from humans and dinosaurs alike. Now an avalanche has blocked their way to their source of food, and the sabertooths are divided over what to do. The only hope for a peaceful solution lies with Redstripe, a sabertooth leader, and Cai, a thirteen-year-old boy. This unlikely pair embarks on a treacherous journey out of the mountains. But they are only a few steps ahead of a human-hating sabertooth and his hungry followers—in a race that could change Dinotopia forever.

THUNDER FALLS
by Scott Ciencin

Steelgaze, a wise old dinosaur, has grown frustrated with his two young charges, Joseph and Fleetfeet. They turn everything into a contest! So Steelgaze sends them out together on a quest for a hidden prize. But someone has stolen the prize, and the two must track the thief across the rugged terrain of Dinotopia. Unfortunately, their constant competition makes progress nearly impossible. It's not until they help a shipwrecked girl named Teegan that they see the value of cooperating—and just in time, because now they must face the dangerous rapids of Waterfall City's Thunder Falls!

FIRESTORM
by Gene DeWeese

All of Dinotopia is in an uproar. Something is killing off *Arctium longevus*, the special plant that grants Dinotopians long life—sometimes over two hundred years! As desperate citizens set fires to keep the blight under control, Olivia and Albert, along with their dinosaur partners Hightop and Thunderfoot, race to find a solution. But Olivia is secretly determined to claim all the glory for herself. In her hurried search for answers, what important questions is she forgetting to ask?

And coming soon...

RESCUE PARTY
by Mark A. Garland

Every day Loro watches caravans of armored Brachiosaurs leave his town and cross the bridge into the dangerous jungles of the Rainy Basin. Someday, he promises himself, he will go with them. Then a deadly storm sweeps over Dinotopia, and the Brachiosaurs help the towns that were hit the hardest. So when a hot-air balloon crashes into the jungle, Loro and his friends know they are the only ones who can help. Loro's dream will finally come true, but can he survive the perils of the Rainy Basin?

REVISIT THE WORLD OF

in these titles,
available wherever books are sold...
OR
You can send in this coupon (with check or money order)
and have the books mailed directly to you!

❑   *Windchaser* (0-679-86981-6) $3.99
     by Scott Ciencin
❑   *River Quest* (0-679-86982-4) $3.99
     by John Vornholt
❑   *Hatchling* (0-679-86984-0) $3.99
     by Midori Snyder
❑   *Lost City* (0-679-86983-2) $3.99
     by Scott Ciencin
❑   *Sabertooth Mountain* (0-679-88095-X) $3.99
     by John Vornholt
❑   *Thunder Falls* (0-679-88256-1) $3.99
     by Scott Ciencin
❑   *Firestorm* (0-679-88619-2) $3.99
     by Gene DeWeese
❑   *The Maze* (0-679-88264-2) $3.99
     by Peter David

Subtotal. . . . . $ _____

Shipping and handling. . . . . $ _3.00_

Sales tax (where applicable). . . . . $ _____

Total amount enclosed . . . . $ _____

Name _____

Address _____

City _____ **State**_____**Zip** _____